"Charles *didn't* ask you to marry him?"

Steffie shook her head.

A look of righteous indignation came over her father's face. "Then I'd best have a talk with that boy. I won't allow him to trifle with your affections."

"Dad!" Steffie had trouble not laughing over the old-fashioned terms he used.

"I mean it, Steffie. I refuse to allow that young man to hurt you again."

"He only has that power if I give it to him—which I won't. You're looking at a woman of the nineties, Dad, and we're too smart to let a man *trifle* with us."

"Nevertheless I'd better have a talk with him."

Her expression might have been outwardly serene, but Stephanie's insides were dancing a wild jig. "You'll do no such thing," she insisted. "I want you to promise you're not going to interfere with Charles and me."

Her father stubbornly refused to answer.

"I'd be mortified if you even bring up the subject of marriage with him."

"But—"

"I'm trusting you, Dad. Now, good night."

Dear Reader,

I'm thrilled and excited that you're reading the ORCHARD VALLEY trilogy. These three books—*Valerie, Stephanie* and *Norah*—come straight from my heart.

I was born and raised in Yakima, Washington, which is often referred to as the apple capital of the world. Huge orchards spread out across the Yakima Valley, and the scent of flowering apple trees fills the air each spring. How well I remember their beauty—and the dread of a late-spring freeze!

I've loosely based Orchard Valley on Yakima and on the small town of Port Orchard, where my husband and I moved several years ago to raise our family. Although I've situated Orchard Valley in Oregon, it could be any small town, anywhere in the United States or Canada. Any small town where there's a sense of community, where people help each other, where neighbors become friends. I hope I've succeeded in capturing that wonderful small-town feeling.

The three sisters in these books are reunited because of a family crisis. There's nothing like the threat of losing someone we love to help us recognize our real values and appreciate our families, our roots. I hope that (like me!) you'll weep with Valerie as she discovers what really matters in life and that you'll sympathize with Stephanie as she deals with her past. And I'm sure you'll cheer with Norah as she meets her match!

I'd be delighted to learn your reactions to the ORCHARD VALLEY trilogy. (In fact, I *always* love hearing from my readers!) You can write to me at P.O. Box 1458, Port Orchard, Washington 98366.

Sincerely,

Debbie Macomber

STEPHANIE
Debbie Macomber

Harlequin Books

TORONTO • NEW YORK • LONDON
AMSTERDAM • PARIS • SYDNEY • HAMBURG
STOCKHOLM • ATHENS • TOKYO • MILAN
MADRID • WARSAW • BUDAPEST • AUCKLAND

ISBN 0-373-03239-0

Harlequin Romance first edition December 1992

STEPHANIE

CHAPTER ONE

HOME.

Stephanie Bloomfield lugged her heavy suitcase up the porch steps of the large white-pillared house. She moved quietly, careful not to wake her two sisters, though it occurred to her that they might be at the hospital.

She herself had spent the best part—no, the worst part, she amended tiredly—of the past two days either in a plane or standing at the counter in a foreign airport. Or was that three days? She couldn't tell anymore.

Norah, her younger sister, had managed to call her in Italy nearly a week ago about their father's heart attack. The connection had been bad and she'd had difficulty hearing Norah, but the sense of urgency had come clearly over the wire. Their father was gravely ill, and Steffie needed to hurry home—something that turned out to be much easier said than done.

Steffie had been living just outside Rome, attending classes at the university. She'd been participating in a special program, learning Italian and studying Renaissance history and culture. For three years she'd traveled effortlessly from one end of the country to the other. Now, just when she desperately needed to fly home, the airports were closed down by a transportation strike that paralyzed Italy. It didn't help that, at the time, she was staying in a small, relatively isolated village hundreds of miles from Rome. She'd been on a brief holiday, visiting a friend's family.

It had taken her several days and what felt like three lifetimes to arrange passage home. *Days,* when it should have been only a matter of hours. This past week had been the most stressful of her life. She'd been in touch with her sisters as often as possible, and at last report heard from Norah that their father was resting comfortably. It wasn't difficult to read between the lines and hear the dread in Norah's voice. Her youngest sister, bless her heart, had never been much good at hiding the truth. Although Norah had tried to sound reassuring, Steffie was well aware that her father's condition had worsened. That was when she'd undertaken the most daring move of her life. She'd made contact with some men of questionable scruples, sold every personal possession of value and, at a hugely inflated price, obtained a means out of the country, by way of Japan, with layovers in places she'd never expected to visit. It was decidedly an indirect route to Oregon, but she was home now. Heaven only knew how much longer it would have taken if she hadn't resorted to such drastic measures.

After a whole day of waiting at the Tokyo airport, fighting for a space aboard any available flight to the States, and then the long flight itself, Steffie was frantic for news of her father. Frantic and fearful. In some ways, not knowing was almost better than knowing....

She opened the front door and stepped silently inside the sleeping house. She'd adjusted her watch to Pacific time, but her mind was caught somewhere between Italy and Tokyo. She was too exhausted to be tired. Too worried to be hungry, although she couldn't remember the last meal she'd eaten.

Setting down her impossibly heavy suitcase, she stood in the foyer and breathed in the scent of polished wood and welcome.

She was home.

Her father's den was to her right, and she immediately felt drawn there. Pausing in the doorway, she flipped on the light switch and stood gazing at the room that was so much her father's. A massive stone fireplace commanded one entire wall, while two other walls were lined with floor-to-ceiling bookcases.

She looked at his wingback chair, the soft leather creased from years of use. Closing her eyes, Steffie breathed in deeply, savoring the scent of old leather and books and the sweet pungency of pipe tobacco. This was her father's room, and she'd never missed him more than she did at that moment.

His presence seemed to fill the den. His robust laugh echoed silently against the walls. Steffie could easily visualize him sitting behind the cherrywood desk, the accounting ledgers spread open and his pipe propped in the ugly ceramic ashtray—the one she'd made for him the summer she'd turned eleven.

The photograph of her mother caught her eye. David Bloomfield could leave his daughters no finer legacy than the love he'd shared with their mother. He'd changed following Grace's death. Steffie had noticed it even before she left Orchard Valley. She'd guessed it from his letters in the years since. And she'd been especially aware of the changes when he came to visit her in Italy last spring. The spark was gone. The relentless passion for life that had always been so much a part of him was missing now. Each month his letters were more painful to read, more lifeless and subdued. Without his wife at his side, David Bloomfield was as empty as . . . as that chair there, his old reading chair, standing in front of the fireplace.

Steffie's gaze slipped to the newspaper spread across the ottoman. It felt as though, any minute, her father would walk through the door, settle back in his chair and resume reading.

Only he wouldn't.

He might never sit in this room again, Steffie realized, her heart constricting with pain. He might never reach for one of his favorite books and lovingly leaf through its pages until he found the passage he wanted. He might never sit by the fireplace, pipe in hand. He might never look up when she entered the room and smile when he saw it was Steffie—his "princess."

The pain in her chest grew more intense and the need to release her emotions burned in her, but Steffie ignored it, as she had a thousand times before. She wasn't a weeper. She'd guarded her emotions vigilantly for three long years. Ever since that night with Charles Tomaselli when he'd—

She brushed the thought from her mind with the efficiency of long practice. Charles was a painful figure from her past. One best forgotten, or at least ignored. She hadn't thought of him in months and refused to do so now. Sooner or later she'd be forced to exchange pleasantries with him, but when she did, she'd pretend she had trouble remembering who he was, as though he were merely a casual acquaintance and not the man who'd broken her heart. That seemed the best way to handle the situation—to pretend she'd completely forgotten their last humiliating encounter.

If he did insist on renewing their acquaintance, which wasn't likely, she'd show him how mature she was, how sophisticated and cosmopolitan she'd become. Then he'd regret the careless, cruel way he'd treated her.

There was a sound in the hallway, and Steffie moved out of the den just as Norah reached the bottom of the stairs.

"Steffie? My goodness, you're home!" Norah exclaimed, rushing to embrace her.

And then, with a small cry of welcome, Valerie, the oldest of the three girls, bounded down the stairs, her long cotton gown dancing about her feet.

"Steff, I'm so glad you're home," Valerie cried, wrapping her arms around both her sisters. "When did you get in? Why didn't you let us know so we could meet you at the airport?"

"I flew standby most of the way, so I wasn't sure when I'd land. I caught the Air Porter and then a cab." She took a deep breath. "I'm just glad I'm here."

"I am, too," Valerie said with an uncharacteristic display of emotion, wiping the tears from her cheeks. Normally Valerie was a model of restraint. Seeing her this shaken revealed, more plainly than anything she could have said, how desperately ill their father was.

By tacit agreement, they moved into the kitchen. Valerie set about preparing a pot of tea. According to the digital clock on the microwave, it was a little past three. Steffie hadn't realized it was quite that late. She could hardly recall the last time she'd slept in a bed. Four days ago, perhaps.

"How's Dad?" It was the question she'd been yearning to ask from the moment she'd walked in the door. The question she was afraid to ask.

"He's doing just great," Norah said, her soft voice rising with delight. "We came really close to losing him, Steffie. Valerie and I were in a panic because things looked bad and Dr. Winston couldn't delay the surgery. And Dad pulled through! But..."

"But he..." Valerie began when Norah hesitated.

"He what?" Steffie prompted. Although she was thrilled with the news that her father had survived the crisis, she couldn't help wondering why both her sisters seemed reluctant to continue. "Tell me," she insisted. She didn't want to be protected from the truth.

"Apparently Dad had a near-death experience," Norah finally supplied.

"But isn't that fairly common? Especially during that kind of surgery? I've been reading for years about people who travel through a dark tunnel into the light."

"I wouldn't know how normal it is to talk to someone in the spirit world, would you?" Valerie snapped.

"Dad claims he talked to Mom." Once again it was Norah who supplied the information.

"To Mom?" Steffie felt numb, unsure of how to react.

"Which we all know is impossible." Valerie hurried barefoot across the kitchen floor to pour boiling water into the teapot. She placed three mugs, three spoons and the sugar bowl on a tray; when the tea had steeped, she filled the cups, obviously preoccupied with her task. Carrying the tray to the table, she served her sisters, then leaped up to get a plate of Norah's home-baked cookies. "I think Dad needs to talk to a counselor," she said abruptly.

"Valerie," Norah sighed as though this were a well-worn argument. "You're overreacting."

"You would, too, if Dad was saying to you the things he says to me." Valerie stirred her tea without looking up.

Norah sighed again. "Dad honestly believes he spoke to Mom and if it makes him feel better, then I don't think we should try to discount his experience."

"What was Mom supposed to have said to him?" Steffie asked, intrigued by the interplay between her two sisters. She helped herself to a couple of oatmeal cookies as she spoke.

"That's what worries me the most." Valerie raised her voice, clearly unsettled. "He's got some fool notion that we're all going to marry."

"Now, that's profound." Steffie couldn't hide her amusement. The three of them were of marriageable age; it made sense that they'd eventually find husbands.

"But he claims to know *who* we're going to marry," Norah said, grinning sheepishly, as though she found the whole thing amusing.

"He's been wearing this silly smile for two days." Valerie groaned, dropping her forehead onto her arms. "He's been talking about a houseful of grandchildren, too. The ones *we're* supposed to present him with—and all in the next few years. If it wasn't so ridiculous, I'd cry."

"Has he said who I'm supposed to marry?" Steffie asked, curiosity getting the better of her.

Valerie lifted her head to glare at Stephanie, and Norah chuckled. "That's something else that's irritating Valerie," she explained. "Dad hasn't told any of us, at least not directly. Not yet."

"He's acting like he knows this wonderful secret and he's keeping it all to himself, dropping hints every now and then. I swear it's driving me crazy."

"I don't mind it," Norah said. To someone else, she might have sounded self-righteous, but Steffie recognized her younger sister's compassion and knew that it edged out any hint of righteousness. "Dad's smiling again. He's excited about the future and even if he's becoming a bit . . . presumptuous about the three of us, I honestly can't say I mind. I'm just so glad to have him alive.''

Valerie nodded, her argument apparently gone. ''I guess I can put up with a few remarks, too.''

''This is the first time one of us hasn't stayed all night at the hospital,'' Norah explained, her mouth curving into a gentle smile. ''Dr. Winston insisted there wasn't any need. Not anymore.''

''Don't be fooled by that guy,'' Valerie muttered under her breath. ''He may look like your average, laid-back country doctor, but he's got a backbone of steel.''

He must have, if Valerie was reacting like this, Stephanie thought with sudden interest. From the sounds of it, her sister had finally encountered a will as strong as her own. So, either Valerie had changed her ways or she had—could it be?—a soft spot for Dr. Winston.

''In other words,'' Steffie said quickly, ''I missed the worst of it. Dad's out of danger now and will eventually recover?''

''Yes,'' Norah said cheerfully. ''Everything'll be back to normal.''

''Not exactly,'' Valerie countered. ''Within a few weeks Dad will be the picture of health, but the three of us will be pulling out our hair after listening to all his talk about marriage, husbands and grandchildren!''

BRIGHT SUNLIGHT poured through the open window of Steffie's bedroom when she woke. The house was quiet, but the sounds of the day drifted in from outside. Birds chirped merrily in the distance and a spring breeze set the chimes on the back porch tinkling and rustled the curtains lightly. She could hear work crews in the orchard—spraying the apple trees, Steffie guessed.

After those long days of struggling to get home, Steffie exulted in the sensation of familiarity. She wrapped the feel of it around her like a warm quilt. The crisis had passed. Her father would survive, and all the world seemed brighter, sweeter, happier.

Reluctantly she slid out of bed and dressed, pulling a pair of slacks and a light sweater from her suitcase.

She found a note on the kitchen table explaining that both Valerie and Norah were at the hospital. They were going to leave her arrival as a surprise, so she could come any time she was ready. There was no need to rush. Not anymore.

Selecting a banana from the fruit bowl on the kitchen counter, she ate that while reheating a cup of coffee in the microwave. As the timer was counting down the seconds, she walked into her father's den and reached for the newspaper, intending to take it with her to the hospital.

She would read it, Steffie decided, to catch up on the local news. But even as she formed this thought, she knew she was lying to herself.

There was only one reason she was taking the local newspaper with her. Only one reason she'd even picked it up. *Charles Tomaselli*. She turned to the front page. The *Orchard Valley Clarion*. She allowed her eyes to skim the headlines for several moments.

Emotion came at her in waves. First apprehension. She'd give anything to avoid seeing Charles again. Then anger. He'd humiliated her. Laughed at her. She'd never forgive him for that. Never. The agony of his humiliation smoldered even now, years later. Yet, much as she wanted to hate Charles, she found she couldn't. She didn't love him any longer. That was over, finished. He'd cured her of love in the most effective way possible. No, she reassured herself, she didn't love him, but she couldn't make herself hate him, either.

She could handle this. She had to. Besides, he was probably as eager to avoid any encounters between them as she was.

Determined now, she tucked the paper under her arm and grabbed the car keys Norah had thoughtfully left on the kitchen table. With the steaming coffee mug in her hand, she headed out the door.

When she arrived at Orchard Valley General, Steffie paused, taken aback by a sudden rush of grief. The last time she'd gone through those doors had been the day her mother died. Steffie's heart stilled at the nearly overwhelming sadness she felt. She hadn't expected that. It took her a couple of minutes to compose herself. Then she continued toward the elevator.

When she arrived at the waiting room, she found Norah speaking to one of the nurses, while Valerie sat reading. It was so unusual to find her older sister doing anything sedentary that Steffie nearly did a double take.

"Steffie!" Norah said, her face lighting when she saw her sister. "Did you get enough sleep?"

"I'm fine." It would take more than one night's rest to recuperate from the past week.

"Did you fix yourself some breakfast?"

"Yes, little mother, I did. Can I see Dad now or is there anything else you'd like to ask me?" She slipped her arm around her sister's trim waist, feeling elated. It was wonderful to be home, wonderful to be with her family.

"You're here," Valerie said, joining them. "Dad asked me earlier when was the last time we'd heard from you. I told him this morning."

"He's going to be moved out of the Surgical Intensive Care Unit some time tomorrow," Norah said happily. "Then we'll all be able to see him at once. As it is now, only one of us can visit at a time."

"Norah, would you like me to take your sister in to see your father?" A plump, matronly nurse had bustled up to them.

"Please," Steffie answered eagerly before Norah could speak. The nurse led her through a hallway with glass-walled cubicles. Every imaginable sort of medical equipment seemed to be in use here, but Steffie barely noticed. She was far too excited about seeing her father. The nurse stopped at one of the cubicles and gestured Stephanie inside.

He was sitting up in bed. He smiled and held out his arms to her. "Steffie," he said faintly, "come here,

Princess.'' He was connected to several monitoring devices, she noticed.

She walked into his hold, careful to stay clear of the wires and tubes, astonished at his weak embrace after the bone-crushing hugs she was accustomed to receiving from him. Her sisters had claimed the spark was back in his eyes. They'd talked about how well he looked.

Steffie disagreed.

She was shocked by his paleness, by the gauntness of his appearance. If he was so much better *now,* she hated to think what he must have looked like a week earlier.

''It's so good to see you,'' her father said, his voice cracking with emotion. ''I've missed you, Princess.''

''I've missed you, too,'' Steffie said, wiping a tear from the corner of her eye as she straightened.

''You're home to stay?''

Steffie wasn't sure how to answer. Home represented so much to her, much more than she'd realized, but she loved Italy, too. Still, just gazing out on the orchards this morning had reminded her how much she'd missed her life in Orchard Valley.

She'd left bruised and vulnerable; she'd returned strong and sure of herself. Being in Italy had helped her heal. But there was no longer any reason to stay away. She was ready to come home.

She'd been trying to decide what to do next when she'd received word of her father's heart attack. Her courses were completed, but remaining in Italy had a strong appeal. She could travel for a while, continue her studies, perhaps do some teaching herself. She could move to some place like Boston or New York. Or she could return to Orchard Valley. Steffie hadn't known what she wanted.

"I'm home for as long as you need me."

"You'll stay," her father insisted with unshakable confidence. "Oh, yes."

"What makes you so sure?"

He smiled mysteriously and his voice dropped to a whisper. "Your mother told me."

"Mom?" Steffie was beginning to appreciate Valerie's concerns.

"Yup. I suppose you're going to act like your sister and suggest I see some fancy doctor with a couch in his office. I did talk to your mother. She sends her love, by the way."

Steffie didn't know what to say. Was she supposed to ask him to convey a message for her? "What did Mom . . . tell you?" she ventured instead.

"Quite a bit, but mainly she said I had quite a few more years left in me. She promised they'd be good ones, too." He paused, chuckling softly. "Your mother always did know I had a soft spot in my heart for babies. And there's going to be a passel of them born in this family within the next few years."

"Babies?"

"An even dozen." The first sign of color crept into his cheeks. "Can you believe it? My little girls are going to make me a grandfather twelve times over."

"Uh . . ."

"I know it sounds like I've got a screw loose, but..."

"Daddy, you think whatever you like as long as it makes you happy."

"It's more than thinking, Princess. It's a fact, sure as I'm lying here. But never mind that now. Let me get a good look at you. My goodness," he said, grinning proudly, "you're even lovelier than I remembered."

Steffie beamed with pleasure. She knew very well that she was no raving beauty, but her looks were nothing to be ashamed of, either. Her dark hair was straight as a clothespin, reaching to the middle of her back. She wore it pulled away from her face, using combs, a style that accentuated her prominent cheekbones and the strong lines of her face. Her eyes were deep brown.

Steffie had just started to regale her father with the adventures of the past week when the same nurse who'd escorted her in to see him reappeared, ready to lead her back to the waiting area.

Steffie wanted to argue. They'd barely had five minutes together! But she forced back her objections; she wouldn't do anything that might upset her father. She kissed his leathery cheek and promised to return soon.

Valerie was waiting for her, but Norah was nowhere in sight.

"Well?" Valerie asked, glancing up from her magazine. "Did he say anything to you about talking to Mom?"

Steffie nodded, secretly a little amused. "He seems downright excited about the prospect of grandchildren. I hate to see him disappointed, don't you?"

"Hmm?" Valerie muttered.

"Since you're the oldest, it makes sense you should be the first," she teased, taking delight in her sister's blank look.

"For what?" Valerie asked.

"To produce a grandchild for Dad. The last time you wrote, I seem to remember you had quite a lot to say about Rowdy Cassidy. Might as well aim high—marry a multimillionaire—even if he is your boss."

"Rowdy," Valerie repeated as though she'd never heard the name before. "Oh... Rowdy. Of course there's always Rowdy. Why didn't I think of him?" With that, Valerie returned to her magazine.

Baffled, Steffie shook her head.

She wandered over to the coffeemaker, poured herself a fresh cup and sat down near her sister. She reached for the newspaper she'd brought with her and opened it to the front page, reading each article in turn. She was relieved to recognize several names; obviously not much had changed while she was away.

Folding back the second page of the weekly paper, she found that her eyes were automatically drawn to the small black-and-white photograph of Charles Tomaselli. For a wild second her heart seemed to stop.

He looked the same. Still as attractive as sin. No man had the right to be that good-looking. Dark hair, gleaming dark eyes. But what bothered her the most was the impact his picture had on her. It wasn't supposed to be like this. She should be free of any emotional entanglement. She should be able to stare at that photograph and feel nothing. Instead she was swamped by so many confused, uncomfortable emotions that she could hardly breathe.

Determined to focus her attention elsewhere, she started on an article with Charles's byline. He'd written an investigative feature, clearly one of a series, about the unhealthy and often unsafe conditions under which many of the migrant workers lived and worked in the community's surrounding apple orchards.

Two paragraphs into the piece, Steffie had to stop reading. She'd come to her father's name, along with the name of their orchard. Obviously Charles hadn't done his research! Steffie knew how hard her parents had worked to ease the plight of the migrant workers. Her mother had set up a medical clinic. And unlike certain other orchard owners, her father had built them decent housing and seen to it that they were properly fed and fairly paid.

Steffie tried to continue reading, but the red haze of anger made it impossible. Her stomach twisted in painful knots as she rose to her feet.

"Valerie," she demanded. "What was Dad doing when he suffered his heart attack?"

"I think Norah said he was sitting on the porch. What makes you ask?"

"He'd been reading the newspaper, hadn't he?"

"I wouldn't know for sure, but I don't think so."

"He must have been!" Steffie declared, walking toward the elevator. She stabbed the button with her thumb, seething at the sense of betrayal she felt. All the evidence pointed to one thing. She'd found the newspaper spread open in his den. Her father had picked up the *Orchard Valley Clarion,* read the article, and then in shock and dismay had wandered onto the porch.

"Steffie, what is it?"

"Have you *read* this?" she asked, thrusting the newspaper in front of her sister. "Did you see what Charles Tomaselli wrote about our father?"

"No, I haven't, but—"

"Look at the date," she said, folding back the front page.

"Yes?" Valerie asked, still sounding confused.

"Isn't that the day of Dad's heart attack?"

"Yes, but—"

"You'd be upset, too, if you'd worked half your life improving the conditions of migrant workers only to have your efforts ridiculed before the entire community!"

"Steffie," Valerie said, gently pressing Steffie's arm. "I can't believe this. Charles is Dad's friend. He's called several times to ask about him. Why, he was even here the night of Dad's surgery."

"He was probably suffering from a large dose of guilt." It seemed perfectly obvious that Charles knew what he'd done. Her father's heart attack had happened the same day the article was published. So Charles *must* have known, must have figured it out himself. And that was why he'd come calling—she was sure of it.

But it was going to take a whole lot more than a few words of concern to smooth over what he'd done. Once Steffie had confronted Charles, she intended to stop off at Joan Lind's office. Joan might be as old as a sand dune, but she was a damn good attorney and Steffie meant to sue Tomaselli for everything he ever hoped to have.

The elevator arrived and she stepped briskly inside.

"Where are you going?" Valerie wanted to know as the doors started to close.

"To give Tomaselli a piece of my mind."

The doors blocked Valerie from view, but her sister's words came through loud and clear. "A piece of your mind? Are you sure you have any to spare?"

BY THE TIME Steffie reached Main Street and located a parking spot, the anger and hurt actually made her feel ill. Her cheeks were feverishly hot. Her stomach churned.

Charles disliked her, and he was taking it out on her father. Well, she couldn't allow him to do it.

She entered the newspaper office, then hesitated. There was a reception desk and a polished wooden railing; it separated the public area from the work space, with its computer terminals, Teletype machine and ringing phones. Beyond it two rows of desks occupied by reporters and other staff lined each side of the room, creating a wide center aisle that led directly to the editor's desk.

She noticed Charles immediately. As the *Clarion*'s editor, he had a work area that took up the entire end of the room. He was on the phone, but his eyes locked immediately with hers. There'd been a time when she would have swooned to have him look at her like this—with admiration, with surprise, with a hint of pleasure. But that time was long past.

Undaunted, she opened the low gate and walked purposefully down the center aisle until she'd reached his desk. She could hear the gate swinging back and forth behind her, keeping time with her steps. By now, Charles clearly understood that this wasn't a social call.

"Brent, let me get back to you." He abruptly replaced the receiver. "Well, well, if it isn't Stephanie Bloomfield. To what do I owe the pleasure of this visit?"

His casual insouciance infuriated her. Steffie slapped the newspaper down on his desk. "Did you honestly think you'd get away with this?" she asked, amazed at the calmness of her own voice.

Charles's eyes steadily held hers. "I don't know what you're talking about."

"You published this piece, didn't you?"

"What article do you mean? I publish lots of pieces."

His attitude didn't fool her. "The one about living conditions among migrant orchard workers. Now, I ask you, who owns the largest apple orchard in three counties? The first paragraph is filled with innuendo, but then you get right down to brass tacks, don't you—by naming my father!"

"Stephanie—"

"I'm not finished yet!" she shouted. In fact, she was just warming up to her subject. "You didn't think any of us would notice, did you?"

"Notice what?" He crossed his arms over his chest as though he'd grown bored with her tirade.

"The date of the article," she said, gaining momentum. "It's the same day as my father's heart attack. The very same day—"

"Stephanie—"

"Don't call me that!" Tears rolled down her face, surprising her. "Everyone calls me Steffie." Roughly, she wiped them away, hating this display of weakness, especially in front of Charles. "I—don't know how you can live with yourself."

"If you want the truth, I don't have much of a problem."

"I didn't think your sort would," she muttered contemptuously. "Well, you'll be hearing from Joan Lind."

"Joan Lind retired last year."

"Then I'll hire someone else," she said, turning on her heel. She marched through the office, slamming the low gate, which had only recently recovered from her entrance.

To her surprise, confronting Charles hadn't eased her pain.

When she pulled out of the parking space, the tires spun and squealed. She felt suddenly embarrassed. She hadn't meant to make such a dramatic exit. Nor was she pleased when she glanced in her rearview mirror to find that Charles had followed her outside.

CHAPTER TWO

WITH THE HURT propelling her, Steffie raced home. In her present frame of mind, she didn't dare return to the hospital. Now wasn't the time to make polite conversation with her sisters, or to meet her father's doctor. Not when she desperately needed to vent this terrible sense of frustration and betrayal.

Charles's treachery cut deep. They'd had their differences, but Steffie had never once believed he would purposely set out to hurt her or her family. She'd been wrong. Charles was both vindictive and unforgiving, and that was more painful than the things he'd said to her that last day they'd been together. That horrible day when he'd laughed at her.

She was shocked that Charles still had the power to make her feel this way, but apparently his grip on her heart was as strong now as it had been three years earlier. The time she'd spent away from home, the time she'd given herself to heal, might never have existed. She was no less vulnerable to him now.

From the first time Steffie met Charles, she'd been fascinated with him. Infatuated. In the beginning, she hoped he returned her feelings. She'd been attending the University of Portland, making the fifty-mile commute into the city each day. Her mother had died a few months earlier, so Steffie had decided against moving into a dorm, as she'd originally planned.

In her sorrow, she'd craved the comfort of familiar people and places. She was worried, too, about her father, who seemed to be walking around in a fog of grief.

Valerie was already living in Texas at that point, and although she'd come home often while their mother was ill, her work schedule had kept her from visiting much since.

Norah, who was in the university's nursing program, used to drive to Portland with her. But Steffie would have made the hour's drive twice a day by herself if she'd had to, simply so she could see Charles more often.

It mortified her now, looking back. Her excuses to see him had been embarrassingly transparent. She'd been so wide-eyed with adoration that she'd repeatedly made a fool of herself.

Her cheeks flamed as she recalled the times she'd followed him around like a lost puppy. The way she'd studied every word, every line, he'd written. The way she'd worshiped him from afar, until her love had burned fiercely within her, impossible to contain or control....

It hurt to remember those times and as she so often had in the past, she blocked the memories from her mind rather than relive the humiliation she'd suffered because of him.

Her anger had cooled by the time she'd finished the ten-mile drive out of Orchard Valley to the family home. Once she arrived, the thought of going inside held no appeal. She needed to do something physically demanding to work off her frustration.

The stables were located behind the house. Valerie and Norah had never really taken to riding, but Steffie, who was the family daredevil, had loved it. The sense of freedom and power had been addictive to a young girl struggling to discover her own identity. Some of the happiest memories she had of her childhood were the times she'd gone horseback riding with her father.

She knew from Norah's letters that he hadn't ridden much lately and had left exercising the horses to the hired help.

The stable held six stalls, four of them empty, and a tack room at the rear. Both Fury and Princess raised their sleek heads when she entered the barn. Princess was the gentle mare her father had purchased and named for her several years earlier; Fury was her father's gelding, large and black, notoriously temperamental. He pawed the ground vigorously as she approached.

"How're you doing, big boy?" she asked, rubbing his soft muzzle. "I'm not ignoring you, Princess," she told the mare across the aisle. "It's just that I'm in the mood for a really hard workout."

After allowing Fury to refamiliarize himself with her, Steffie collected saddle and bridle from the tack room. She slipped on Fury's bridle, then opened the stall gate and led him out. The gelding seemed to be just as eager to run as she was to ride, and he shifted his weight impatiently as she tightened the girth and adjusted the stirrups.

Leading him out of the stable, she'd set her foot in the stirrup, ready to mount, when she noticed a small red sports car racing down the driveway. It didn't take her two seconds to recognize Charles.

Steffie had no intention of speaking to a man she considered a traitor. In fact, she didn't want to ever see him again. She planned to talk to her sisters, then seek legal counsel. Charles would pay for what he'd done to her father, and she'd make sure he paid dearly. Even if he retained bitter feelings about her, that was no reason to take vengeance on her family.

Reaching for the saddle horn, she hoisted herself onto Fury's back. She hadn't used a Western saddle since she'd left home and needed a few moments to get used to it again. Fury scampered in a side trot as Steffie changed her position, leaning slightly forward.

"It's all right, boy," she assured him in a calm, quiet voice that belied her eagerness to escape—and leave Charles behind.

She ignored his honk and although it was childish, she derived a certain amount of pleasure from turning her back on him. She nudged Fury's side and with her chin at a haughty angle, trotted away.

She'd only gone a short distance when she became aware that Charles was following her. Fury didn't need any encouragement to increase his steady trot to a full gallop. Although she was an experienced horsewoman, Steffie wasn't prepared for the sudden burst of speed. Fury raced as though fire was licking at his heels.

Holding on to the reins, Steffie adjusted herself as well as she could, bouncing and jolting uncomfortably, unable to adapt herself to Fury's rhythm. She'd ridden in Italy, but not nearly as often as she would have liked and always with an English-style saddle. Not only was she out of practice, she hadn't the strength to control a horse of Fury's size and power—especially one who hadn't been exercised much lately. She should have thought of that, she groaned. Thank goodness he was familiar with the terrain. He galloped first along the dirt road, bordered on both sides by apple trees. He kicked up a cloud of dust in his wake, which made it impossible for Steffie to tell whether Charles had continued after her. She prayed he hadn't.

Only when Fury took a sharp turn to the left, through a rough patch of ground, did Steffie see that Charles was indeed behind her. She tried to pull in the reins, to slow Fury down to a more comfortable trot, but the gelding had a mind of his own. Next she tried to talk to him but her hair flew about her face, the long ends slapping her cheeks, blinding her. Between her bouncing in the saddle and the hair flapping in her face, she didn't manage a single intelligible word.

By now she had a lot more than Charles to worry about. She was about to lose what little control she had of the horse. And on this rough ground, she feared for the animal's safety, not to mention her own.

Steffie remembered the land well enough to realize they were headed for a bluff that overlooked the valley. It was at the farthest reach of her family's property, and a place Steffie had often gone when she needed to be alone. She approved of Fury's choice, if not his means of getting there.

Her one consolation was that it would be virtually impossible for Charles to follow her any farther. His vehicle would never make it over the rock-strewn landscape. With no other option, he'd be forced to turn back. Or wait. And if he chose to wait by the side of the dirt road, he'd be out of luck—she'd simply take another route home, connecting with the road at a different point.

Once they reached their destination, Fury slowed to a canter. Steffie pulled back on the reins, slid out of the saddle and commanded her trembling legs to keep her upright. She wiped the sweat from his neck and rubbed him down with a handful of long dry grass, then led him to a gentle stream. She was loosely holding the reins, allowing him to drink the clear, cool water, when she noticed a whirl of dust. Thinking at first that it might be a dust devil, she only glanced in that direction. Her heart sank all the way to her knees when she made out the form of a red sports car.

It wasn't possible. The terrain was far too uneven and rocky. Charles must be out of his mind to risk the undercarriage of his car by racing after her.

Squaring her shoulders, she turned to face him, refusing to give one quarter. Charles bounded out of the

small car like a spring being released. She nearly
flinched at the hard, angry set of his face.

"What the bloody hell do you think you're doing?" he demanded—as though he had a right to ask.

Steffie didn't acknowledge him but resumed her
rubdown of the horse.

"You might have been killed, you idiot. And you
might have killed that damn horse, too."

It was in her mind to tell him that she was no idiot,
but she refused to become involved in a shouting
match. And she *did* feel guilty about taking out a
horse she couldn't control—her father's horse, yet.
But Charles was a traitor, and worse. The next time
she spoke to him, Steffie thought angrily, it would be
through an attorney.

It looked for a moment as though he intended to
grip her by the shoulders; in fact, what she heard him
mutter sounded like a threat to "shake some sense"
into her. He raised his hands, then briefly closed his
eyes and spun away from her.

"You haven't changed a bit, have you?" he cried,
jerking one hand through his hair as he stalked toward his car.

Still Steffie remained silent, although she had to bite
her tongue in an effort not to lash back at him. He'd
purposely hurt her family, hurt her. There was nothing left to be said.

Abruptly he yanked his car door open. Steffie
blinked at the unexpectedness of his withdrawal. She
wasn't sure what he'd planned to do, but this swift
capitulation came as a surprise.

Not wanting him to assume she cared about his actions one way or the other, she tried to ignore him. She looped Fury's reins around a low branch and walked away, too. Her legs were trembling so badly that she decided to climb onto a boulder. Perched there, she gazed out at the sweeping view of the valley below, jewel-like in its green lushness.

Charles's footsteps behind her announced that he hadn't left, after all.

"Read it!" he shouted, slapping the very newspaper she'd given him against her thigh. "*This* time finish the article."

Steffie gasped, then pressed her lips together, tilting her head to avoid looking at him.

"Fine, be stubborn. That's nothing new. But if you won't read the article, I'll do it for you." He grabbed the newspaper.

Steffie wanted to blot out every word, but she refused to resort to anything quite as juvenile as plugging her ears. She cringed inwardly as his strong voice read the opening paragraph. On hearing it a second time, she felt the piece sounded even more hostile to her father than she'd believed earlier. It was as though Charles had taken the very heart of David Bloomfield's accomplishments and crushed it with falsehoods and accusations.

By the time he reached the spot where Steffie had stopped reading, where her father's name was actually mentioned, the anger inside her had rekindled. She closed her eyes to the wave of pain that threatened to swallow her.

He read on, and she waited with foreboding for the attack she knew was coming. But it didn't happen. As Charles continued, she suddenly realized how wrong she'd been. How *terribly* wrong. Her heart in her throat, she turned toward him. Charles went on, reading a direct quote from David Bloomfield in which he told of the changes he'd made over the years to aid migrant workers.

At first Steffie was convinced she'd misunderstood. Nor was she entirely sure she could believe Charles. He might be making it up as he went along, she thought wildly, instead of actually reading the article. She reached for the newspaper and snatched it away from him.

It only took her a moment to locate the paragraph he'd just read. He hadn't made it up! There, bold as could be, was the quote from her father, followed by two long paragraphs that reported the progressive measures the Bloomfield Orchards had implemented over the years.

Her stomach plummeted, and she began to feel as though she were sitting in a deck chair on the *Titanic*. That feeling intensified as she finished reading the article. Because she soon discovered that not only was her father quoted—approvingly—several times, but their family orchard was used as a model for other local orchards to follow.

Steffie drew in a deep, stabilizing breath before she looked up at Charles. Once again, she'd made a fool of herself in front of him. She cringed in acute embarrassment and self-contempt. Oh, Lord, what a jerk she'd been. What a total jerk.

She'd known that meeting Charles again was inevitable. She'd hoped that on her return he'd view her—from afar, of course—as mature and sophisticated. She'd wanted him to see her as cosmopolitan and cultured, unlike the lovesick twenty-one-year-old who'd left Orchard Valley three years before.

She'd imagined their first meeting. She would step forward, a gentle smile on her face, and hold out her hand politely. She'd murmur ever so sweetly that it was lovely to see him again, but unfortunately she couldn't recall his name. Charles Something-or-other, wasn't it?

"It looks like I owe you an apology," she said instead, her voice quavering a bit despite her efforts to keep it even.

"You're damn right you owe me an apology!" he flared back. "I'd assumed you might have changed in three years. Instead you're an even bigger...nuisance."

His words felt like a slap across the face, and she flinched involuntarily. There wasn't a thing she could say in her own defense, nothing that would take away the shame of what she'd done. No words would erase the way she'd come into his office and created a scene in front of his entire staff.

"So it seems," she said as steadily as her crumbling poise would allow.

"You scared the hell out of me, taking off like that," he raged. "You might have killed yourself."

Again, there was nothing she could say. Had she been in any other frame of mind, she would have recognized that with a horse like Fury, she was heading for trouble.

"You're a crazy woman!" he shouted, his anger fully ignited now. "How do you think I would have felt if you'd been hurt? What about your father? You accuse *me* of causing his heart attack! What do you think would've happened to him if you'd killed yourself?"

"I—I..." Hating the telltale action, she bit her lip to stop its trembling.

"Damn it all," he shouted and to Steffie's dismay, he reached down and pulled her to her feet. His hands clasped her shoulders and he drew her into his arms.

Before she had time to react, she was completely caught in his embrace, her hands trapped against his heaving chest.

One hand left her shoulder and slid into her long, tangled hair.

"Do you even have a clue what I was thinking?" he whispered. "Do you have any idea what was going through my mind?"

Her heart thundered. She should fight her way out of his embrace. She should demand that he release her, tell him he had no right to take her in his arms. But Steffie couldn't make herself move, couldn't make herself speak.

She didn't try to stop him even when it became obvious that he was going to kiss her. Mentally she braced herself, knowing he was angry, suspecting that he intended to punish her with a savage kiss.

As so often of late, Steffie was wrong. When his mouth found hers, it was a gentle brushing of lips. Her eyes opened in wonder and surprise.

Charles kissed her again, longer this time, his mouth gliding over hers, and staying there. Before she realized what she was doing, she moved her arms upward and timidly locked them behind his neck. Her lips parted to his and he pressed her closer.

But only for a moment. "No, Steffie," he said in a raw whisper, gripping both wrists and breaking her hold. He stepped back as though he'd been scorched. Their gazes held for several seconds before he turned and hurried away.

He left as abruptly as he'd arrived, his sports car spitting dirt and small stones as he roared off. She sighed and prepared to mount Fury for the long journey home.

STEFFIE TOOK a long nap that afternoon, waking sometime in the early evening. The sun was setting, dousing the orchards in a lovely shade of soft pink. Not knowing what time it was, she came downstairs to find Norah humming softly in the kitchen.

"Hi," Norah greeted her, smiling brightly when she saw Steffie. "I was beginning to wonder if you'd ever wake up. You must have been exhausted."

Steffie nodded.

"There's a plate for you in the oven. I bet you're famished."

The last thing she'd eaten had been that banana at breakfast. Murmuring her thanks, she walked across the room and removed the plate from the oven. Her sister had always been a good cook and Steffie gazed longingly at the broiled chicken breast, new red potatoes and fresh green beans.

"Where'd you go this morning?" Norah asked cheerfully, continuing to wash dishes. "Valerie said you seemed upset over something to do with Charles Tomaselli?"

Steffie pulled out a stool at the counter and sat down to eat. "I needed to ask him something."

"Did you get everything settled?"

Steffie lowered her gaze. "Everything's clear now."

"Good. He really has been wonderful through all this. Dad's pleased with how well the article on migrant workers was received. You read it, didn't you? The two of them spent weeks collecting facts, and Dad actually did a bit of undercover work. It was the first time since Mom died that he revealed much interest in anything. I don't think even Charles knows how much Dad put into that piece. He must have gone over every detail a dozen times."

Steffie, who was just about to begin her meal, promptly lost her appetite. "I—I didn't realize that."

"I was planning to mail you the article, but then Dad had the heart attack and everything else fell by the wayside," Norah explained conversationally, leaning against the counter as she dried her hands.

"Where's Val?"

"In the den. She's working. You know Val—she's as dedicated a businesswoman as anyone's likely to meet. Within a few days of arriving home, she'd ordered a fax machine so she could get files and stuff from the office. Although I have to admit her mind hasn't been on the job lately."

"Oh?" Steffie made an effort to taste her meal. The chicken was tender and delicious. She took a second bite.

Norah wiggled her eyebrows playfully. "In case you hadn't noticed, there's a romance brewing between Val and Dr. Winston."

"There is?" Steffie asked, fork poised in midair. "What about Valerie's boss? Every time I got a letter from her it was Rowdy this and Rowdy that."

"I don't know about Rowdy, but I do know what I saw the night of Dad's surgery."

"Which was?" Steffie asked anxiously.

"Valerie came apart after we were allowed to go in and see Dad. She didn't realize I knew how upset she was, but I figured she needed a few minutes alone. I hadn't seen Dad yet myself, and when I did, I could understand Valerie's concern. He was very close to death. I don't know how much anyone's told you about Dad's condition, but it's a miracle he survived the open-heart surgery. Anyway," she said with a sigh, "when I went in to see Dad I wondered if he'd last the night. I know Colby didn't think he would. Neither did any of the others who were on the surgical team. Naturally, they didn't say as much, but I could tell what they were thinking. I've worked in surgery often enough myself to know who's likely to survive and who isn't. One look told me we'd be lucky if Dad lasted another few hours, although I was encouraged that he'd survived the surgery itself. There were plenty of complications, with fluid in his lungs and all."

"Tell me about Valerie," Steffie urged.

"Oh, yeah, Valerie. Well, after she'd been with Dad she went out onto the patio outside the surgical waiting room. She was crying, which we both know is rare for Val. I could tell she needed someone. When I got back from seeing Dad, I started to go out to her, thinking we'd be able to comfort each other, but I stopped when I saw that Colby was with her."

Steffie had heard wonderful things about Dr. Winston already, but his compassion for her sister confirmed everything she'd come to know of him. She said so to Norah, who nodded.

"They were sitting together and he was holding her in his arms. I don't know how to explain it, but he had this...look. As though he would've done anything within his power to take away her pain. I thought right then that he had the look of a man who's just discovered he's fallen in love."

"And Valerie?"

"I think she might have realized they were in love with each other before Colby did. You know how strong Valerie is, how she never wants to let anyone do anything for her. Well, for the first time since I can remember, she needed someone and Colby's the person she turned to."

"Valerie and Dr. Winston," Steffie said slowly. She'd often wondered what it would be like when her oldest sister fell in love. Valerie had always been so pragmatic, much too sensible to become involved in a relationship while she was in college. She was there to be educated, not to find a husband, she'd told Steffie.

"Then Dad took a turn for the better," Norah went on, "and he started all this talk about us marrying and having kids. I'm afraid Valerie's taking it much too seriously, worrying about it too much. But then, she's in love for the first time in her life and she's frightened half to death that Colby's the wrong man for her. Or more to the point, that she's the wrong woman for him."

"Love is love, and if they both feel so strongly, then what's the problem?"

Norah's smile was sad and a bit hesitant. "Colby's as traditional as they come. He's looking for more than a wife—I think he wants a woman straight out of the 1950s."

"Valerie knows this?"

"Of course she does. Colby's well aware of the kind of woman Valerie is, too. Her calling isn't the kitchen, it's the boardroom."

"I say more power to her." In Steffie's opinion, Colby Winston should appreciate her sister's God-given talents.

"Exactly!" Norah agreed, "but if Valerie marries Colby she'd probably have to quit her job. For one thing, CHIPS doesn't have a branch in this part of the country. And she's worked too hard and too long to let go of her career."

"In other words, they'd both have to compromise—and they can't?"

"Exactly. No one ever told me love could be so complicated. I feel sorry for them both. They couldn't be more miserable."

Steffie finished off the last of the small red potatoes, not wanting her sister to guess how curious she was about her father's "chat" with her mother. "What do you think of all this talk about Dad's... experience?"

Norah pulled up a stool and sat across from Steffie. "I don't know. *He* believes he actually talked with Mom and that's what's important, don't you think?"

Steffie wasn't sure of anything anymore. She'd once been confident that she knew what she wanted in life. Then everything had fallen apart. But the time she'd spent in Italy had helped her regain a perspective on her own life... hadn't it?

It suddenly occurred to Steffie with a sense of horror that she'd spent three years studying and traveling in Europe, and her primary purpose had been *to impress Charles Tomaselli* when she returned.

She'd impressed him, all right, by making an even bigger fool of herself than before.

"Dad's been talking about his grandchildren all afternoon," Norah continued, breaking into Steffie's thoughts. Actually Steffie was grateful for the intrusion.

"Grandchildren," she repeated softly. "From you, naturally?" She couldn't imagine Valerie as a mother, and she herself had no intention of marrying. When her father was well enough to come home, Steffie intended to find herself an apartment in Portland and to apply for a fellowship and begin her doctorate. She'd completed her master's in Italy after an intensive language program, and in her last year there, she'd taken several advanced courses. It was hard to believe someone so well educated could be so dismally unaware of her own motives, she mused unhappily.

"Dad claims I'm going to present him with six grandchildren," Norah said, barely restraining a smile. "Can you imagine me with six children?"

"Which means Valerie's going to be responsible for another six."

"No, three. According to Dad's rumblings, you're going to have three of the little darlings yourself."

Steffie grinned, despite her depression. The picture of herself married and with a brood of children was somewhat amusing. She'd only loved one man in her life and the experience had been so painful that she was determined never to repeat the mistake.

"I guess we'll see," Steffie said, sliding off her stool to carry her now-empty plate to the sink.

"I guess we will," Norah concurred.

Although she'd slept for a good part of the afternoon, two hours later Steffie was yawning. Making her excuses, she returned to her bedroom, showered and got into bed, savoring the crisp, clean sheets.

Sitting up, her knees tucked under her chin, she pondered her conversation with Norah. In the years since she'd moved away, a number of her friends had married. She'd gotten wedding invitations, passed on by Norah, every few months. And several of her high school and college friends were already mothers, some two times over.

While she was in Italy, Steffie hadn't allowed herself to think about anything more pressing than her studies, which had occupied most of her time. She'd traveled and studied and worked hard. But at odd moments, when she received a wedding invitation or a birth announcement, she'd occasionally taken a moment to wonder if her life was missing something. Or when she was with Mario, the adorable young son of her landlady in Rome, she'd imagined, more than once, how it would feel to have a family of her own.... She'd usually managed to suppress the yearning quickly.

And now she was experiencing it again, and more sharply than ever before. All this talk of weddings and children troubled her. She felt excluded, somehow. In the end, Valerie would probably marry her Dr. Winston, and there'd be a wonderful man for Norah, she was sure of it.

But for her? She found she couldn't believe in the same kind of happy ending.

CHAPTER THREE

ALTHOUGH SHE WAS exhausted, Steffie couldn't sleep. After tossing about restlessly and tangling her sheets, she sat on the edge of the bed and pushed the long hair away from her face.

She'd prefer to think the nap she'd taken that afternoon was responsible for this inability to sleep.

But she knew better.

She couldn't sleep because her thoughts wouldn't leave her alone. The memory of what a fool she'd made of herself with Charles hounded her until she wanted to scream.

With graphic clarity she recalled the first time she'd heard of Charles Tomaselli. She'd read his introductory column in the *Clarion* and had loved his wit and style. No matter what she thought of him now, she could never fault his talent as a writer. Charles had a way of turning a phrase that gave a reader pause. He chose his words carefully, writing in a clear, economical manner that managed to be both clever and precise. And he had a wide range of subjects, covering everything from social trends to the local political scene.

When she'd read his first few columns, she'd assumed he was much older, because the confidence of
his observations and his style suggested a man of con-
siderable experience. It wasn't until several weeks later
that she actually met him. At the time she'd been so
dumbstruck she could barely put two words together.

She'd tried to tell him how much she enjoyed his
editor's column, but the words had twisted on the end
of her tongue and came out sounding jerky and odd,
like something a preschooler might say.

She'd been terribly embarrassed, but Charles had
responded graciously, thanking her for the compliment.

It wasn't just the fact that he was in his late twen-
ties—and not his fifties—that had taken Steffie by
surprise. Nor was it the fact that he was strikingly
handsome, although he was certainly easy on the eyes,
with his dark Italian looks. What struck Steffie like a
fist to the stomach was the instant and powerful attraction she felt for him.

Unlike Valerie, who'd gone out on only a handful
of dates through high school and college, Steffie had
had an active social calendar. She'd always been well
liked by both sexes—popular enough to be voted
Prom Queen her senior year of high school. But although she had lots of friends who happened to be
boys, Steffie had never been in love. She'd thought,
more than once, that she was, but she'd been wise
enough to realize she was only infatuated, or in love
with the idea of being in love.

Although she was twenty-one, she'd never been involved in a serious relationship. She hadn't considered herself ready for one—until she met the newly appointed editor of the *Orchard Valley Clarion.*

When she met Charles, she knew immediately that she was going to love this man. How she could be so certain was unclear, even to her, but to the very depths of her young heart, she was absolutely convinced of it.

Following that initial meeting, Steffie had driven home in a daze. She didn't tell anyone, including her sisters, what she felt. She didn't know how she could possibly explain her feelings without sounding silly. Love at first sight was something reserved for movies and romance novels.

She'd been filled with questions, wondering if Charles had felt it, too; she soon persuaded herself that he had.

He was older, twenty-seven she discovered, amazingly mature and sophisticated, while she was an inexperienced third-year college student.

Steffie lived for the next edition of the *Clarion,* ripping open the newspaper until she found his column, and devoured each word Charles had written. Occasionally he wrote a feature article, and she read those just as avidly. She soon discovered that others were equally taken with his work. He'd been in town for less than two months and had already become a source of pride and pleasure to the entire community.

Steffie straightened and reached over to turn on her bedside lamp. Obviously she wouldn't be able to sleep, and sitting in her room, dredging up memories of Charles, wasn't helping.

The house was dark and silent, which meant Valerie and Norah were both asleep. Not wanting to wake either of her sisters, Steffie slipped quietly down the dimly lit stairs.

She thought about making herself a cup of tea, then decided against it. Instead, she tiptoed into her father's den. She turned on a soft light and reached for *Sonnets from the Portuguese*—an especially lovely edition her father had given her mother years ago, before they were married. Steffie cuddled up in his reading chair, already comforted.

The leather felt cool against her skin. An afghan her mother had knitted when the girls were still young lay neatly folded on the ottoman. Valerie must have brought it in with her, since it hadn't been there the night before.

Steffie reached for the rose-colored afghan and tucked it around her, then turned to one of her favorite poems.

She might have made it through two pages, maybe even three, before her mind drifted back to Charles. Back to that first year...

He hadn't noticed her. Hadn't shared the instant attraction. In fact, he hadn't even remembered her name. Steffie was stunned. She'd dreamed of him every night since the day they met. Wonderful dreams of laughing and loving, of strolling hand in hand through the apple orchard, sharing secrets and planning the rest of their lives. Her heart was so full of love that it was all she could do not to tell him outright.

Getting a man to notice her was a new challenge to Steffie. Until then, it had always been the other way around. The men—no, *boys*—had been the ones to seek her out. For the first time in her life, Steffie found herself at a disadvantage in a relationship. Clearly the only option open to her was to let Charles know as subtly as possible that she was interested. It shouldn't be such a difficult task for a former Prom Queen.

Except that it was...

The first thing Steffie did was to write him a letter commending his writing ability and his opinions. She'd agonized over every word, then waited for nearly two weeks for a reply.

There hadn't been one.

Charles hadn't printed her letter and didn't respond, either. Steffie had been crushed. Never one to quit, though, she'd visited the newspaper office with suggestions for a wide variety of stories. As she recalled, she'd managed to come up with 150 such ideas. Admittedly some were better than others.

Charles had been polite, but had made it plain that although he appreciated her suggestions, he already had an enthusiastic staff whose job it was to come up with regional stories.

Her plan had been for Charles to be so awed by her concern about local issues and her invaluable ideas that he'd invite her to dinner to discuss her interest. Although, in retrospect, it sounded terribly naive, she'd actually believed this would happen.

Apparently, she spent more time than she realized hanging around the newspaper office and making a nuisance of herself because Charles unexpectedly asked her out for coffee one morning.

Steffie had been so excited that she could barely sit still. She was further encouraged when Charles chose a booth in the farthest, most private corner of the local coffee shop.

Even now, three years afterward, Steffie could recall how thrilled she'd been. She'd slid into the red vinyl seat across from him, sure he could read all the love and adoration in her eyes.

The encounter, however, proved to be a bitter disappointment for Steffie. Charles had been kind, but firm. He couldn't help noticing, he'd said, how much time she spent at the newspaper office, and was sure her studies must have been suffering. He'd also gotten her letter and the other notes she'd sent him, and although he was flattered by her attention, he was much too busy with the paper to become involved in a relationship.

When Steffie had pressed him for more of an explanation, he'd told her without a second's pause that he considered her too young to date. Furthermore, he felt she was . . . too innocent.

Having recently turned twenty-one, Steffie was aghast at his lack of foresight. She was a mature woman, and six years' difference in their ages was unimportant. If she didn't object, then he shouldn't, either.

As an active member of her high school debating team, Steffie had learned how to argue, and now she'd used every skill at her disposal.

It didn't work.

He'd finally told her she was a nice *kid* but he simply wasn't interested. That he was a busy man and didn't have the time or the patience to be a baby-sitter. A baby-sitter! He wasn't exactly impolite, but it was clear he had no intention of asking her out. Ever.

Their coffee had just been served, and Charles hadn't taken more than a sip of it before he tossed some money on the table and left.

Steffie had remained there, too hurt to breathe, too numb to feel anything more than a painful kind of disappointment. She couldn't remember how long she'd sat in the booth. Long after her coffee had cooled, she knew.

Obviously she'd sat there much too long because she had decided with a sigh of relief that Charles Tomaselli was obviously lying.

"STEFF."

The gentle voice was followed by a warm hand on her shoulder.

"What are you doing sleeping down here?"

Steffie raised her head and blinked. Valerie, dressed in a long housecoat, stood beside her.

"What time is it?"

"Morning," Valerie said with a smile. "How long have you been here?"

Moving her legs, Steffie winced at the unexpected discomfort. She wasn't sure how long she'd been asleep, but her legs were stiff and sore and the book still lay open on her lap.

"I was going to fix myself a cup of coffee and some toast before heading to the hospital. Do you want some?"

"Please." She worked one shoulder and then the other and rotated her neck, hoping to ease the crick. Her thoughts had been so full of what had happened between her and Charles in those early days that she couldn't remember falling asleep. It surprised her that she had. She wondered if her musings had followed her into her dreams, then decided it would be better if they hadn't.

"I can't tell you how good Dad looks compared to a week ago," Valerie said when Steffie joined her in the kitchen. "It's like a miracle."

"It was so crazy being stuck in Italy like that."

"You know—" Valerie paused, clutching a large earthenware mug "—in a way I'm grateful you couldn't get home for a while. It might be the one thing that kept Dad alive. He was determined to see you before he died."

Steffie wasn't sure she followed her sister's thoughts. "Do you mean to say Dad had a means of controlling the timing of his . . . demise?"

"Sort of. Death was what he wanted. If I've learned anything through all this, it's that the human will is an amazing thing."

Steffie began making toast, bringing the butter and Norah's homemade strawberry jam out of the refrigerator. "I'm not sure I understand what you mean about the human will."

"I don't know if I can explain it," Valerie said after a moment, her look distant and thoughtful. "All I know is that Dad was on the brink of death for days. When I first arrived, Colby explained that Dad would require open-heart surgery. He wanted to perform the operation immediately but couldn't because of a variety of complications Dad was experiencing. If you want the medical terms for all this you can ask Norah or Colby, but basically it boiled down to one thing. Dad had lost the will to fight for his life. He's been miserable without Mom. We both know that, but I don't think anyone fully appreciated exactly how *lonely* he's been."

"I shouldn't have left him." Despite Valerie's immediate reassurances, Steffie partially blamed herself for her father's failing health. She'd known when he came to visit her in Italy last year that something was wrong. He'd taken the trip to Europe not out of any desire to travel but because Valerie and Norah had thought it would help revive his spirits. The fact that Steffie was living in Italy had been a convenient excuse.

Steffie had enjoyed the time with her father, and had been excited about showing him the country she'd come to love and introducing him to her new friends. She'd carefully avoided any conversation having to do with Orchard Valley or her mother. Her father had urged her to come home, but she'd already registered for new courses and paid her rent in advance and planned another trip. All excuses. Because it really came down to one thing: she'd been afraid to go home.

Steffie Bloomfield afraid! The family daredevil. Dauntless, reckless Steffie Bloomfield was afraid of a mere man. More precisely, she was terrified of having to speak to Charles again, of looking him in the eye and pretending it didn't hurt any longer. Pretending she didn't love him. Pretending she didn't feel humiliated.

She was incapable of shrugging off the past, especially when it was much simpler just to stay in Europe. She loved her history courses, she enjoyed traveling throughout Italy, she was fond of her landlady's family, she had lots of friends and acquaintances. She'd discovered, too, that she had a real aptitude for languages; besides being proficient in Italian, she'd picked up some French and German and hoped to continue learning them. No, she had decided, there were far too many good reasons to remain in Europe. And so she'd stayed.

"Do you want to ride into the hospital with me?" Valerie asked, apparently deep in her own thoughts.

"Sure."

"I might need to do a few errands later, but you might be able to get a ride home from Norah if I'm not back."

"I'm not worried. I haven't been able to spend much time with Dad yet." Steffie felt guilty about rushing out of the hospital the day before without returning to see him.

As it turned out, Steffie couldn't have chosen a better morning to be with her father. It was the day he was being transferred out of the Surgical Intensive Care Unit and onto the surgical ward. His time in the SICU was a short four days, his recovery nothing short of remarkable. Even Dr. Winston seemed to think so.

"I can't get over how beautiful you've become," her father said when he woke from a short nap. Steffie was sitting at his bedside, doing the *New York Times* crossword puzzle and feeling downright self-satisfied that she'd managed to fill in a good half of the answers.

"I'll tell you what I've become," Steffie said with a laugh, "and that's Italian. The first day after I left Rome I slipped from English to Italian and then back again without noticing. I think I spent twice as long clearing customs as anyone else, simply because the agent didn't know what to make of me."

"So can you cook me some real Italian spaghetti?" her father asked.

"I certainly can, and I promise it'll be so good you'll dream about it the rest of your life."

"With plenty of garlic?"

Steffie raised the tips of her fingers to her lips and made a loud smacking sound. "With enough garlic to ward off vampires for the next hundred years. Besides, I hear garlic's good for your heart."

"But lousy for your love life."

"I don't think either of us needs to worry about that," she teased.

"Ah." David Bloomfield shook his head. "That's where you're wrong, Princess. You, my darling Stephanie, are about to discover what it means to be in love."

Steffie didn't have the heart to say she already knew all she cared to on that subject. *Thanks, Dad—but no thanks,* she told him silently. Falling in love wasn't an experience she wanted to repeat.

"You aren't going to argue with me the way Valerie did, are you?"

"Would it do any good?"

"No," he said, smiling broadly.

"I didn't think so."

"You don't believe I actually talked to your mother, do you?"

"Uh . . ." It wasn't that she disbelieved him exactly. *He* was convinced that something had happened, so her opinion was irrelevant. He claimed to have enjoyed a lengthy conversation with her mother while strolling around some celestial lake. Valerie had mentioned it almost immediately after Steffie's arrival home. Norah had talked about it, too. Steffie found their accounts fascinating. Did she believe it had really happened? She didn't know. She was inclined to think he'd experienced some kind of revelation, all right—but whether it was spiritual, as he thought, or a dream, or a fantasy of his own making, she had no idea. And it didn't matter.

"You won't be the only one who doesn't believe my talk with your mother was real."

"It isn't that, Dad."

"Don't you worry about it. Time will prove me right."

"Prove you right about what?" a distinctive male voice asked from behind her. Steffie froze and the dread washed over her like a huge wave.

Charles Tomaselli.

He was the last person she'd expected to meet here. The last person she wanted to see again.

"How're you feeling, David?" he asked.

"I've been better."

"I'll bet you have," Charles said wryly.

Steffie was on her feet immediately. "I'll leave you two to chat," she said with a cheery lilt, anxious to leave the room.

"There's no reason for you to go," her father countered, holding out his hand to her. "Your smile is the brightest sunshine I've seen in days. Isn't that so, Charles?"

Steffie cringed inwardly, and not giving Charles time to comment, quickly squeezed her father's hand. "I don't think it's a good idea for you to have too much company all at once."

"She might be right," Charles agreed. "Besides, I've got some business to discuss with you. I thought you'd be interested in hearing what happened as a result of that article we did on the migrant-worker situation."

Steffie's breath caught in her throat until she realized Charles wasn't referring to the stunt she'd pulled in his office the day before. She went weak with relief when she heard him mention something about Commissioner O'Dell initiating an inspection program.

Steffie still hadn't looked at Charles, still hadn't turned to face him. She delayed it as long as possible, leaning forward to gently kiss her father's cheek. "I'll get a ride back to the house with Valerie or Norah, but I'll be in again this evening and we can finish our... discussion."

"I'll see you then, Princess."

Steffie nodded and mentally braced herself as she turned away from her father's bed. She looked shyly at Charles. It amazed her how their eyes instantly met, how they were drawn to gaze at each other, as though neither could resist the pull of mutual attraction. Her own heart gave a small burst of joy and she wondered if, deep within, his did, too.

"Hello, Steffie."

"Charles." Her voice was low and wispy. "I'll see you later, Dad."

"Bye, Princess."

Her gaze skidded past Charles as she hurried from the room, eager now to make her escape. By the time she was at the end of the corridor, her heart was roaring and she was breathless—all because of a casual encounter with Charles. Obviously she'd need to prepare herself mentally for even such minor confrontations.

She hadn't been nearly as shy with him that summer three years earlier, she remembered with chagrin. It mortified her now to think of her brazen behavior...

If Charles considered her a *kid* when he'd invited her for coffee, then Steffie decided she owed it to herself to prove him wrong. Without difficulty, she'd been able to discover where Charles lived. Crime had never been much of a problem in Orchard Valley, and Charles had been kind enough to leave his front door unlocked.

By the time he appeared several hours later, there were scented candles lit throughout the living room and a bottle of champagne chilling in the kitchen.

"Is that you, darling?" Steffie had called out from the bathroom. She'd been sitting in a bubble-filled tub for the better part of an hour, and her skin had started to shrivel. She was also worried about the candles dripping and the champagne getting warm, but she dared not leave, fearing she'd never be able to adjust the bubbles again. It was important that he think she was completely nude, though in reality she wore a skimpy bikini.

Charles didn't answer. He stalked into the room, stopping abruptly in the doorway as his shocked gaze fell on her.

"What the hell are you doing here?" he'd demanded.

"I thought it was important for you to know I'm not a child."

"Then what are you—a mermaid?"

She forced a soft laugh and said in what she hoped was a sultry, adult voice. "No, silly man, I'm a *woman* and if you'll come here, I'll prove it to you."

"Get out."

"Out? But... but I was hoping you'd join me."

"No way, sweetheart. Now either you remove yourself from my home or I'm calling the police."

She pushed her big toe under the water tap. "I think my toe might be stuck."

"Fine, I'll call the plumber."

"But Charles, darling..."

"Charles, nothing," he snapped, marching into the bathroom and gripping her by the upper arm. The force of his strength lifted her halfway out of the tub. She screeched, stumbling to find her balance. As soon as she was upright, Charles tossed a towel at her and told her she had five minutes to leave before he called the police.

Steffie had fled, but she'd seen the gleam of male admiration in Charles's eyes, seen the way he'd looked at her for a second or two. And, fool that she was, she hadn't been the least bit discouraged. Instead, she'd devised yet another plan.

STEFFIE WANDERED into the waiting area searching for Valerie. One of the orderlies mentioned that her sister had gone to pick up office supplies. Steffie remembered hearing something about an errand, but she hadn't been paying enough attention to recall whether Valerie was returning to the hospital or going straight home.

Oh, well, there was always Norah.

Tracking down her youngest sister didn't take long. Within five minutes, Steffie found her in the emergency room—preparing to go on duty. The hospital was understaffed, and now that their father was beginning to recover, Norah had returned to work. Steffie didn't bother to ask for a ride.

Hoping Charles would be gone, she returned to the surgical ward. Her luck hadn't improved, and they met at the elevator.

"I thought you were headed home?"

"I'll have to wait for Valerie," she said, preparing to edge past him. "Or try to get a cab."

His arm blocked her escape. "There's no need to do that. I'll drop you off at the house."

"No, thanks," she returned stiffly.

"I want to talk to you, anyway," he said, none too gently guiding her into the elevator. "And as they say, there's no time like the present."

"This really isn't necessary, Charles."

"Oh, but it is."

She noticed, when he led her out of the hospital to the parking lot, that he was driving the same red sports car she'd seen the day before. It eased her conscience a bit that it hadn't been damaged during his free-for-all race across the countryside.

He opened the door for her, and Steffie climbed inside. She was adjusting the seat belt when Charles joined her. The space seemed to shrink like silk pressed against a hot iron. Their shoulders touched, their thighs, their arms. For a moment, Steffie held her breath.

"You said you wanted to talk to me?" she said after he'd pulled out of the hospital parking lot. She was leaning as close to the passenger door as she could.

"I thought we'd discuss it over a glass of iced tea. You did plan on inviting me inside, didn't you?" He turned and grinned at her, that boyish, slightly skewed grin she'd always found so appealing.

She'd planned to tell him she had no intention of letting him in; instead she cleared her throat and said, "If you'd like."

"I would."

The ten-mile drive to the house generally took fifteen minutes. Steffie could have sworn Charles was purposely dragging out the time, driving well below the speed limit. They were so close in the small cramped car that she couldn't avoid brushing against him, even though she tried not to. She was trying to forget that he'd kissed her the day before, and this didn't make it any easier! She was trying not to wonder what it would be like to experience his kiss a second time. . . .

Steffie closed her eyes. It was all she could do not to shout at him to hurry. Why was he prolonging these moments alone? The least he could do was make polite conversation.

"My father seems downright cheerful, doesn't he?" If Charles wasn't going to say something, then she would. Anything to ease this terrible awareness.

"He certainly does."

"He's got a reason to live now, and that's made all the difference in the world. I'm not sure what to think about his dream, but—"

"What dream?"

"Uh . . . nothing . . . it's not important." Steffie couldn't believe what she'd done. In her nervousness, in her eagerness to fill the silence, she'd blurted out what should never have been shared.

She relaxed when Charles turned off the road onto the mile-long family driveway. He parked in front of the house.

Steffie didn't wait for him, but threw open her door and jumped out, her keys already in her hand. She had the front door open by the time he caught up with her, and tossing her purse onto the hall table, led him briskly into the kitchen.

Norah had made some iced tea that morning. Steffie silently thanked her sister for her thoughtfulness as she took out the cold pitcher. It didn't take more than a couple of minutes to find two tall glasses, add ice and slice a fresh lemon. Another minute, and the drinks were ready.

"What was it you wanted to say?" Steffie finally asked, leaning against the counter. She hadn't realized how warm she was and she held the glass between both hands, enjoying the coolness against her palms.

"It's about what happened yesterday," Charles said, walking away from her. He paused at the bay window that overlooked the backyard. Just beyond his view was the stable. "Or more appropriately, what shouldn't have happened."

CHAPTER FOUR

"I'D RATHER NOT discuss it," Steffie said adamantly. She didn't want to hear any more about her irresponsible accusations and rash actions. Nor did she wish to hear how much Charles regretted kissing her.

"If anyone needs to apologize, it's me," she said quickly. "Why don't we just leave it at that? I was wrong."

Charles's back was to her as he stared outside toward the stables. "I don't think anyone's ever infuriated me this much," he said quietly. He turned, set his glass of iced tea aside and thrust his hands into his pockets. "I've never met a woman who manages to irritate me the way you do."

Steffie stiffened. "I've already apologized for leaping to conclusions. I admitted I was wrong." She shrugged elaborately. "My only excuse is that I spent a hellish week trying to get home and I haven't slept properly in days and I—"

"This isn't necessary," he said, interrupting her. "I'm not looking for an apology... Actually I'm here to make my own. I want you to know I'm sorry about chasing after you. It was a dangerous thing to do. I might have spooked Fury into throwing you."

"Not to mention damaging your car."

"True enough."

"Let's put it behind us," Steffie suggested with a weak smile. "I was wrong to run away. It was... childish."

"You were angry, too."

"I've never met a *man* who manages to irritate me the way you do," she said, consciously echoing his words.

"We always seem to get on each other's nerves, don't we?" His grin was warm and gentle, just as his kiss had been. Strangely, Steffie found his smile just as devastating.

"We certainly have a history of annoying one another." It took her more courage than he'd ever know to mention the past. But suddenly she hoped they could put that behind them, too.

"I'd never be able to forgive myself if anything had happened to you."

"I wasn't really in any danger of Fury throwing me." Okay, so that was a slight exaggeration, but she *had* remained in the saddle.

"It was a hell of a way for us to meet again." Charles's voice was husky. He moved closer to her and she lowered her gaze, but not before she noticed how his attention seemed to center on her mouth. "There's one thing I'm not sorry about." He took another step toward her and raised his hand to touch her cheek. His fingers brushed aside a stray lock of hair. Steffie found she couldn't move. She couldn't think coherently. She could barely breathe.

"I don't regret kissing you," Charles whispered.

Then Steffie did move. Trembling, she stepped backward and bolted to the other side of the room.

"Stephanie?"

"Call—call me Steffie," she stuttered. Her hands were shaking so badly that she jerked them behind her.

"I prefer to call you Stephanie. You're not a little girl anymore."

She smiled brightly. Now was the perfect time to convince him how sophisticated she'd become after three years in Europe, sophisticated and *experienced*. She was sure that was the type of woman he expected, the type of woman he wanted.

"As kisses go, it certainly was nice," she agreed in an offhand manner. Was she overdoing it? she wondered. "Yours had a gentleness, and that surprised me. Most men aren't like that, you know? When they kiss a woman it's hot and sweaty; they leave a girl breathless."

"I see," Charles said, raising one eyebrow.

She placed her hands on her hips, fashion-model style, and tilted back her head, letting her long brown hair swing lightly. "I'm not the same person I was three years ago. You're right about that. I'm all grown up now."

"So it seems."

"I appreciate the ride home," she said, walking out of the kitchen. She hoped Charles would follow her because she wasn't sure how much longer she could maintain this performance.

"Is there anything else these ... hot, sweaty men taught you?" he asked in a dispassionate voice. He reached for his iced tea, apparently disinclined to leave quite so soon.

She turned around and smiled serenely. "You'd be surprised." Deciding to give him the answer he deserved, she rashly went on. "As you know, I met men of all nationalities—students from all over Europe— and I sampled my fair share of kisses." Mostly chaste kisses of greeting or farewell, but he didn't have to know that. And then there were Mario's exuberant hugs ... Mario was only four years old, but Charles didn't have to know that, either.

Charles scowled then, and set his glass down on the counter hard enough to slosh liquid over the edges. He stalked past her. "Goodbye, *Steffie*," he said coldly, throwing the words over his shoulder.

It wasn't until he'd slammed the front door that she understood that his words had been meant as an insult. He was telling her he'd changed his mind, reconsidered. He'd seen through her little dramatization and decided he'd been wrong, she wasn't an adult. She remained a foolish, immature girl.

STEFFIE WANDERED between two rows of budding apple trees, contemplating her latest disaster with Charles. The setting sun cast a rosy splendor over the orchard. As a girl, Steffie had often walked out here when she needed to think. This was where she found peace, and a tranquillity that eased her burdens. Since her last meeting with Charles, there'd been plenty of those. And regrets. She hadn't seen him in several days and that helped. But it also hurt. There were so many unanswered questions between them, so many unspoken words.

Hearing footsteps behind her, Steffie turned to find Norah walking toward her.

"You've got to do something!" Norah moaned.

"About what?" she asked when Norah moved three agitated paces ahead of her.

"You've got to help Valerie. You're older than I am. You've had more experience with men."

Steffie suppressed the urge to laugh at the irony of this statement, considering her ludicrous performance in front of Charles. She reached up to run her fingers along the smooth bark of a branch. "What's wrong with her?"

"She's making the biggest mistake of her life," Norah said dramatically. It wasn't often that her little sister sounded so distraught. Unfortunately Steffie was hardly the ideal person to advise Valerie on romance.

"I told you before that Valerie and Dr. Winston are in love," Norah continued. "Everyone around them can see it. And whenever Valerie and Colby are together, they can't keep their eyes off each other."

"Then what's the problem?"

"They aren't seeing each other anymore."

"What do you mean?"

"They're avoiding each other. I don't think they've talked in days."

Norah's words struck a chord in Steffie. She knew exactly what Valerie was doing, because she was guilty of the same thing herself. She hadn't seen Charles since the day he'd driven her home from the hospital. They were obviously taking pains to avoid each other—just like Valerie and Dr. Winston.

"I don't see what I can do," Steffie muttered.

"Talk to Val," Norah argued. "She might listen to you."

"What am I supposed to say?"

Norah hesitated, frowning. "I don't know, but you'll think of something. I've given it my best shot and nothing seems to influence her, but you know Valerie . . . I just wasn't getting through to her. Maybe you can."

"I'm glad you have so much faith in my abilities," Steffie said lightly.

"I do have faith in you," Norah said, her blue eyes serious. "You're different now than before you left."

"Three years in Italy will do that to a girl." As she had with Charles, Steffie strived to sound flippant and worldly.

"I don't mean that. You're more thoughtful. More—I don't know—mature, I guess. Before you left Orchard Valley it seemed that you had to prove yourself to the world, but it isn't like that now. I can't see you doing some of the crazy things you used to do."

Just as well that Norah didn't know about some of her "mature" behavior these past few days. And thank heaven no one in the family had any idea of the embarrassing stunts she'd pulled trying to attract Charles's attention three years ago.

"I remember the time you stood on Princess bareback and rode around the yard. You were lucky you didn't break your neck."

Steffie remembered the incident well. It had been shortly before their mother died. She'd been grieving so terribly and doing something utterly dangerous had helped vent some of her pain and grief. But Norah was completely right. It had been a foolish thing to do.

"Okay, I'll talk to Valerie," Steffie promised, "but I don't know how much good it'll do."

STEFFIE TRIED. But the conversation with her sister hadn't gone as planned. One look at Valerie told her how much her sister was suffering. Valerie tried to hide it, but Steffie knew the signs from her own limited experience with love.

They'd become involved in a lengthy discussion about love, then decided neither one of them was qualified to advise the other. They'd thought of bringing Norah in on the conversation but that suggestion had resulted in a bout of unexpected giggles. They couldn't ask Norah about falling in love because she was too busy dating.

One interesting detail that emerged from their talk was something Valerie mentioned almost casually. While Steffie was struggling to find a way home, Charles had seemed very concerned about her. He'd even pulled a few strings in an effort to find her when she didn't arrive on schedule.

Although they'd never openly discussed her relationship with Charles, Valerie seemed to know how

Steffie felt. It wasn't that Steffie had tried to conceal it; with one breath, she admitted how she'd made a fool of herself over the newspaper article and with the next, she'd asked her sister about falling in love. Valerie was certainly astute enough to figure out Steffie's feelings for Charles.

DAVID BLOOMFIELD was now recuperating at home and doing well. Steffie still hadn't seen Charles. She'd thought maybe he'd be stopping by the house to visit her father, whose release from the hospital had been a festive event.

Steffie was pleased to see that Valerie and Colby were able to steal a few moments alone that afternoon, but she didn't think their time together had gone well. They'd gone for a walk in the orchard; Valerie had looked pale and sad when they returned, and Colby had remained silent throughout the celebration dinner that followed.

Knowing it was inevitable that she'd see Charles again, Steffie tried to mentally prepare herself for their next meeting.

She couldn't have guessed that it would be at the local gas station.

"Why, Steffie Bloomfield," Del of Del's Gas-and-Go greeted her when she went inside to pay for her fill-up and buy a bottle of soda. "I swear you're a sight for sore eyes."

She laughed. Del was pot-bellied and close to sixty, but he had to be the biggest flirt in town. "It's good to see you again, too. What do I owe you for the gas?"

"If I were a rich man, I'd say the gas was free. Looking at your pretty face is payment enough. Right, Charles?"

It always happened when she was least prepared, when seeing him was the last thing she expected.

"Yeah, right," Charles answered from behind her with a decided lack of enthusiasm.

"Hello, Charles," she said, turning around to greet him, trying to sound casual and slightly aloof. She pasted a smile on her face, determined not to let him fluster her as he had every single time they'd encountered each other.

"Stephanie."

"I don't know if you heard, but Dad's home now."

"I got word of that the other day." Charles took his wallet out of his hip pocket and paid for his gas.

Steffie twisted the top off her soda and took a deep swallow. It tasted cool and sweet, bringing welcome relief to her suddenly parched throat. "I was thinking you might stop by and visit." *Hoping* more aptly described her thoughts, but she couldn't admit that.

He didn't answer as he followed her outside. The service-station attendant was washing her windshield and Steffie lingered, wanting to say something, anything, to make a fresh start with Charles.

"As I recall, you wrote one of your first columns about Del's, didn't you?"

"You've got a good memory," Charles said, his words a bit less stiff.

The boy had finished with her windows and there was no further excuse to dawdle. Reluctantly she opened her car door. "It was good seeing you. Oh, by the way, Valerie told me you made several efforts to find me when I was trying to get home from Italy. I appreciate all the help you gave my family."

He shrugged. She set one foot inside the car, then paused and glanced back at Charles. She *had* to say something. "Charles." He turned around again, a surprised expression on his face. "There's something you should know."

"What is it?"

"I'm very grateful for your friendship to my family—and to me." With that she ducked inside her car, heart racing, and drove off without looking back.

UNFORTUNATELY dinner that evening was a strained affair. Norah had come to Steffie an hour before with the news that Colby had dated another nurse, a friend of Norah's, three nights running. Norah didn't know whether to tell Valerie, and had asked Steffie's advice.

Steffie thought it best not to say anything to their sister until Norah had slept on the matter.

But Steffie suspected that Valerie was already aware of it, suspected that Valerie knew it in her heart. Although her sister hadn't said anything to the family, Steffie believed she'd quietly made arrangements to return to Texas and her job as vice president of CHIPS, a software company based in Houston.

Everyone could feel something was wrong, but no one said a word during dinner. Everyone was terribly polite—as though the others were strangers—which only heightened the tension.

Their father had made his excuses, claiming to be especially tired, and with Norah's help retired to his room almost immediately after dinner.

Apparently Valerie wasn't in the mood for company either, because she excused herself and retreated to her bedroom, leaving Steffie and Norah to their own devices.

After they'd finished with the dinner dishes, Norah left to attend a wedding shower for a friend.

Feeling at loose ends, Steffie inspected the kitchen. On impulse, she decided to make the spaghetti sauce she'd promised her father. She dragged out the largest pot she could find and began to assemble ingredients. Fresh tomatoes, onions, tomato paste, garlic. No fresh herbs, so dried would have to do. Oh, good, a bottle of nice California red . . .

Humming to herself, she slipped a tape of Verdi's *Aida* in the cassette player and turned up the volume until the music echoed against the kitchen walls. The emotional intensity and dramatic characterizations of the Italian composer suited her mood.

She found an old white apron her father had used years before whenever he barbecued. Wrapping it around her waist, she drew the long strings around to the front and tied them.

Half an hour later, she was stirring the last of the tomato paste into the pot. She added a generous amount of red wine, all the while singing at the top of her lungs. The sound of someone pounding at the back door jolted her back to reality.

Running barefoot across the kitchen, she pulled open the door and saw Charles standing there, holding a pot of purple azaleas.

"Charles! What are you doing here?"

"No one answered the front door," he remarked dryly.

"Oh. Sorry." She walked to the counter to turn off her cassette player. "Come in." The silence was nearly deafening.

"I thought you said your father was home from the hospital?" As though self-conscious about holding a flowerpot, he handed it to Steffie.

"He is," she said, setting the plant aside. "How thoughtful. I'm sure Dad will love this."

"It isn't for David."

"It isn't?"

"No, I was . . . we just got a full-page ad from How Green Is My Thumb Nursery and I felt it might be a gesture of good faith to buy something. I thought you'd appreciate an azalea more than your father would."

Steffie wasn't quite sure what to say other than a soft "Thank you."

He shrugged, apparently eager to leave. He stepped toward the door and she desperately tried to think of something to keep him there, with her.

"Have you eaten?" she asked quickly, even though the sauce was only just starting to simmer and wouldn't be properly ready until the following day.

"What makes you ask?"

"I was just putting together a pot of spaghetti sauce. Dad asked me to cook him something Italian and...well, if you wouldn't mind waiting a bit, I'll be happy to fix you a plate. It really needs to simmer longer, but I know from experience that it's perfectly edible after an hour." She sounded breathless by the time she'd finished.

"I've already had dinner, but thanks, anyway," Charles told her. "I could do with a cup of coffee, though." He nodded toward the half-full pot sitting beside the stove.

"Sure...great. Me too. I'd get Dad but he's sleeping," she explained as she poured him a cup, then one for herself.

"Through that?" Charles motioned toward the cassette player.

"Sure. He loves listening to the same music as I do. Besides he's way over on the other side of the house. I doubt he could even hear it." She didn't mention that a tragic love story was sure to suit Valerie's mood, though. And since her sister's bedroom was directly above the kitchen she was most likely to have been the one serenaded.

Charles cradled the mug in both hands and walked over to examine her efforts. "So you learned to cook while you were away?"

"A little," she admitted.

"I wouldn't have guessed you were the domestic sort." He stirred the sauce with a wooden spoon, lifted it out of the pot and tasted it, using one finger. His brows rose. "This is good."

"Don't sound so surprised."

"There must have been some Italian man you were hoping to impress."

The only man she'd ever wanted to impress was the one standing in the kitchen with her right that moment.

"I was too busy with my studies to date much," she admitted, dumping the empty tomato-paste cans in the garbage.

"That isn't the impression you gave me the other day."

She hesitated, her back to him. "I know. I certainly seem to make a habit of playing the fool when I'm with you."

Charles's voice was rueful. "I've occasionally suffered from the same problem."

The unexpectedness of his admission caught her off balance, and she twisted around to face him. For a long, unguarded moment she soaked in the sight of him.

"There wasn't anyone I dated more than a few times," she told him in a raw whisper.

"Surely there was someone?"

She shook her head. They gazed silently into each other's eyes, and Steffie seemed to lose all sense of time.

Charles was the one who broke the trance. "Uh, your pot seems to be boiling."

"Oh, darn, I forgot to turn down the burner." She raced across the kitchen, flipped the knob on the stove and stirred the sauce briskly, praying it hadn't burned.

While she stood at the stove, Steffie basked in a glow of unfamiliar contentment. It felt so wonderful to be with Charles—not fighting or defensive, not acting like a love-struck adolescent. For the first time, she was truly comfortable with him.

"I'm sure the sauce will be fine," she murmured, picking up her coffee mug.

He pulled out the chair and sat.

As she was getting cream, sugar and teaspoons, she thought she heard some noise from upstairs. Glancing at the ceiling, she frowned.

"Is something wrong?"

Steffie joined him at the table, adding only cream to her own coffee and pushing the sugar bowl toward Charles. "I'm worried about Valerie," she said frankly. "So is Norah. Everyone is, except Dad, which is for the best—I mean, he's got enough on his mind healing from the surgery. He shouldn't be worrying about any of us."

Charles added a level teaspoon of sugar to his coffee, then paused, the spoon held above his cup. "How'd you know I use sugar?"

Her gaze skirted away from his. "We had coffee together once before, remember?"

"No" came his automatic response.

Steffie preferred not to dredge up the unhappy memory again, especially since *he* didn't even seem to recall it. She stared down at the table. "It was the first time you asked me to—you know, leave you alone."

He scowled. "The first time," he repeated, then shook his head in apparent confusion. Just as well, Steffie thought to herself, astounded that he had absolutely no recollection of an incident she remembered in such complete and painful detail.

She decided to change the subject. "Norah baked some cookies the other day, if you'd like some."

Charles declined with a shake of his head. "Tell me what's going on with your sister." His eyes darted to the ceiling.

Steffie wasn't sure how much of Valerie's dilemma she should confide in him, but then remembered Norah's telling her that Charles had been with them the night of her father's surgery. More than likely he knew how Colby and Valerie felt toward each other.

"She's in love," she said after a moment.

"It's Doc Winston, isn't it?"

Steffie nodded. "They seem to have fallen hard."

"So what's wrong?"

Steffie wasn't sure she could explain, when she didn't entirely understand it herself. So she shrugged and said, "I think Colby wants her to be something she can't. Valerie's an incredibly gifted businesswoman. But I gather he wants a woman who'd be happy to stay home and be a housewife—there's nothing wrong with that, of course, but it just isn't right for Valerie. It doesn't look like either one of them is going to compromise."

"If she loves him, maybe she should be willing to compromise first," Charles said, then sipped his coffee. "Take the first step."

"What about Colby? Why does it always have to be the woman who compromises? Don't answer that, I already know. Women have been forced to adapt to men's fickle natures for so many generations that it comes to us naturally. Right?"

Charles was silent for a moment. "I didn't come here to argue about your sister."

"I know, it's just that I found your statement so—" She stopped in midsentence because she didn't want to fight with him, either. They'd done so much of that. And she didn't want this encounter to end the way all the others had.

"I'm sorry," she said. "I'm concerned about her, and I can't help feeling a bit defensive. I'm pretty sure she's making arrangements now to return to Texas— and I wish she wouldn't."

"You haven't had much time with her, have you?"

Steffie tapped the mug with her spoon, staring into the dregs of her coffee. "That's not the whole reason I wish she'd stay." She was silent a moment. "Leaving your problems behind simply doesn't work. Not unless you've exhausted every possibility of reaching a compromise. In fact, I think leaving can make everything much worse. The problem is, I can't tell Valerie that. It's one of those painful realities we each need to discover on our own, I guess. I'm going to talk to her, but I doubt it'll do any good."

Charles's dark eyes were sympathetic. "I hope she listens."

Steffie thanked him with a smile. "I hope she does, too, but the three of us seem to share a wide streak of stubbornness."

Charles rubbed his eyes, and she realized for the first time that he must be exhausted. "You won't get an argument out of me," he said with a tired grin.

"Are you still working as many hours?"

He nodded. "Fifty to sixty a week. We're published twice weekly now and eventually we're looking to go daily. Some days I feel like I'm married to that paper."

The word "married" seemed to hang in the air. At one time Steffie had been convinced beyond any doubt that they'd be married, she and Charles. It was this unshakable resolve that had created so many difficulties in her relationship with Charles. Naively, she'd assumed that all she had to do was *show* him they were meant to love each other and after a few short object lessons, he'd be sure to agree. Now she knew that life—and love—didn't work that way.

"Are you still a jack-of-all-trades with the paper?" she asked, remembering that his job meant he had his hand in every aspect of publishing the weekly newspaper—from writing, editing and layout to distribution.

"Some. We're on a computer system now, which makes everything a lot easier. No more of that cutting and pasting."

"Do you still have an intern?"

Charles relaxed against the back of his chair and nodded. ''Wendy. She's a junior at the University of Portland.''

A red light went on in front of Steffie's eyes. ''What happened to Larry? I thought you were working with him?'' The thought of Charles spending long hours with an attractive college student filled her with a sense of dread.

Then it came to her. She didn't need to worry about competing for Charles any longer.

She was out of the running.

CHAPTER FIVE

"IS SOMEONE HERE?" Steffie heard her father even before he entered the kitchen. He was wearing his plaid housecoat, cinched at the waist, which emphasized the weight he'd recently lost. His white hair was rumpled from sleep.

"David, hello," Charles said, standing to shake hands with him. Her father slowly made his way to the table, declining Charles's gesture of assistance.

"I thought you were still asleep," Steffie said with a loving smile. She'd missed the worst of the crisis, but her sisters had repeatedly told her how close they'd come to losing their father. Now, every time she was with him, she experienced a sense of renewed love and gratitude that his life had been spared.

"How do you expect a man to sleep with such delicious smells coming from the kitchen?" David grumbled good-naturedly. "I swear it's driving me to distraction."

"It's my Italian spaghetti sauce."

Her father squinted. "But we already ate dinner."

"I know. The sauce needs to simmer for several hours and it's even better if you let it sit overnight. I was hoping to surprise you tomorrow night."

Her father nodded approvingly. "Sounds great, Princess." Then he grinned at Charles. "Good to see you, boy."

"You too, old man."

It was apparent that they'd often bantered like this. The atmosphere was relaxed, one of shared affection and camaraderie.

"You were in the neighborhood and decided to stop by?" David inquired. It wasn't likely Charles would come this way except to visit the Bloomfields, and they all knew it.

"I stopped in to check up on you," Charles said, but his gaze drifted involuntarily toward Steffie. Their eyes met briefly before she looked away.

"That's the only reason?" her father pressed.

"I, uh, brought that for Stephanie," he said and pointed in the direction of the potted azalea.

"You wouldn't by any chance happen to be sweet on my little girl, would you?"

"Dad," Steffie broke in urgently, "how about something to drink? Coffee, tea, a glass of water?"

"Nothing, thanks. I just came to see if I was dreaming about garlic and basil or if this was the real thing. I'll leave the two of you to yourselves now." He stood awkwardly, as though he wasn't quite steady on his feet. Steffie's instincts were to help him, but she knew it was important that he do as much as possible on his own. She stepped back, ready to assist him if it became necessary.

Charles was apparently thinking the same thing because he stood beside her, a concerned look on his face.

"I'll see you to your room," she said. The effort of rising from his chair and walking a few paces seemed to deplete her father's strength.

"Nonsense," he objected. "You've got company. Charles isn't here to visit me. I heard him say so himself. That was just an excuse so he could bring you that pretty flower."

"Don't argue with me, Daddy."

Her father grumbled, but allowed her to wrap her arm around his waist to support him. She looked over her shoulder at Charles. "I'll only be a minute."

"Take your time."

No sooner were they out of the kitchen than her father came to a halt, wearing the most delighted grin Steffie had ever seen. "What's so amusing?" she asked.

"Nothing," he said. Then he started chuckling softly. "It's just that your mother was right about this, too. Surprises me, but it shouldn't."

"What? Right about what?"

"You and Charles."

"Daddy, there's nothing between us! We're barely friends."

"Perhaps, but all that's about to change. Soon, too. Very soon."

Her father continued to mutter under his breath, as pleased as ever. Steffie closed her ears to his remarks, knowing that he had to be referring to his dream—the time he'd supposedly spent tiptoeing around the afterlife, gathering information. It hadn't bothered her nearly as much when he was going on about Valerie and Colby, but now that it was her turn, she was decidedly uneasy.

"Charles isn't here to see me," she insisted. "Bringing me the azalea didn't mean anything. He got a new advertising account, that's all. I'm sure he intended to give it to you, but you were sleeping."

"Whatever you say, Princess."

Arguing wouldn't do either of them any good, and besides, she didn't want to keep Charles waiting. She suspected he'd be leaving soon, anyway. Her father sat on the edge of his bed, his eyes frankly curious as he gazed up at her. "I might have guessed. I wasn't sure what to think when your mother mentioned you and Charles. She told me you've been in love with him for quite some time. She's right, isn't she?"

Steffie kissed his brow and ignored his question. "Do you want me to tuck you in?"

"Good heavens, no. You hurry back to your young man. He's waiting for you. Has been for years."

"Good night, Dad."

Her father's grin broadened. "By golly, your mother was right," she heard him mutter as she left the room. "I should have known. Forgive me, Grace, for doubting."

Outside the bedroom door, Steffie started to tremble. Without directly saying so, her father was telling her what she'd most dreaded hearing, and at the same time what she desired above all.

Whether it was the result of fantasy, intuition or, as he believed, spiritual intervention, he'd become convinced that she'd be marrying Charles. The same way he was so certain about what would happen between Valerie and Colby Winston. And Steffie wasn't any more confident about her older sister's relationship than she was of her own with Charles.

"You look like you've seen a ghost," Charles told her when she rejoined him in the kitchen.

She raised her eyes to his, dismayed that he'd noticed. She needed to sit down. He was right, it *had* been a scare, listening to her father talk like that about the two of them, making marriage sound imminent.

"What is it? Is your father all right?"

She nodded. "Oh, he's fine, growing stronger every day..."

"It's good to see him smile again."

Steffie nodded and glanced at the simmering pot of sauce. Anything to keep her gaze away from Charles.

"What's really wrong?" he asked her softly. His concern was gentle and undemanding, and it touched her heart. This was the man she'd always known him to be. The man she'd fallen in love with three years ago—the man she'd never been able to forget.

Had it been anyone else, she would have laughed off her father's words. She would have told her "destined" husband-to-be in a humorous fashion how her father was bent on playing matchmaker.

She couldn't do that with Charles, not when she'd so blatantly played the role herself. He'd assume, and not entirely without justification, that she was up to her old tricks.

"It's nothing," she said, forcing herself to smile brightly. "I can't help thinking how lucky we are to have him with us again."

Charles studied her intently. "You're sure there's nothing wrong?"

"Of course." She looked at him in what she hoped was a reassuring manner.

"If there's anything I can do..."

"There isn't." She smiled, to take the bite from her words. "You've already done so much. We're all indebted to you...you've been wonderful."

"You make me sound like some saint. Trust me, Stephanie, no one's going to canonize me—especially with the things I'm thinking this minute." He was behind her before she even realized he'd moved. His hands were on her shoulders and he gently drew her back and wrapped his arms about her waist. His mouth nuzzled her neck and he breathed in deeply, as though to drink in her scent.

Deluged with warm sensation, Steffie closed her eyes and savored the moment. She'd never believed this could happen. She dared not believe it even now.

It would be so easy to turn into his arms, to bury herself in the comfort he offered. She'd dreamed of this for so long. But now that it was here, she was afraid.

Her hands folded over his, which were joined at her middle. "I—the flowers are..."

"A gesture of good faith."

His words confused her. He must have sensed the uncertainty in her because he spoke again in a low voice, his words reassuring. "Let's start all over again, shall we? From the beginning."

"I—I'm not sure I know what you mean."

He softly kissed the side of her neck, then released her and turned her around so they were face-to-face. "Hello there, my name's Charles Tomaselli. I understand you're Stephanie Bloomfield. It's a real pleasure to meet you." He held out his hand to her, which she took. If his eyes hadn't been so serious, she would have burst into peals of laughter.

"Charles, you say? Anyone ever call you Charlie?"

"Hardly ever. Anyone ever call you Steffie?"

"Only when I was much younger," she teased. "A mere kid."

"I understand you're only recently back in town. I don't suppose you've had time to notice, but there've been a few changes in Orchard Valley. How about if I drive you around, show you the place?"

She hesitated. "When?"

"No time like the present."

"But we've only just met."

"I'm hoping that won't stand in your way. It shouldn't. I'm completely trustworthy."

"Then I'll accept your kind invitation."

"Do you want to bring a sweater?" he asked.

She shook her head.

He reached for her hand, his fingers entwined with hers as he led her toward the front door. It felt like the most natural thing in the world for them to be together.

They bounded down the stairs, carefree and laughing. Charles opened the car door for her, helped her inside and without warning leaned forward to kiss her. Their lips met briefly, then lingered. When he broke away, Charles seemed surprised himself. Steffie glanced up at him, thinking she might read some sign of regret in his eyes, but there was none. Only a free-flowing happiness that reflected her own feelings exactly.

"WHERE WERE YOU last night?" Norah asked late the following morning. "I came home from Julie's wedding shower and you were nowhere to be found."

Steffie spread a thin layer of her sister's strawberry jam across her English muffin. "I went out for a while." She didn't add any details because her father was sitting at the table, lingering over his cup of coffee and the morning newspaper. He might make all the wrong assumptions if he knew she'd been with Charles.

They'd spent nearly two hours driving around the area. Charles had taken her past several new businesses, including fast-food restaurants and some specialty boutiques. He'd shown her the recently constructed six-plex movie theater, a new housing complex and a brand-new mall on the outskirts of town. The drive had been highlighted by an ongoing commentary that included the latest gossip.

Steffie hadn't enjoyed herself so much in a long time. Charles had been entertaining and fun, and he seemed to take pains never to refer to their past differences.

It was late when they'd gotten back to the house, but they sat in the car for another thirty minutes, talking, before Steffie went inside.

She'd fully expected to lie awake half the night savoring the time she'd spent with him, but to her astonishment, she'd fallen asleep almost immediately.

"Steffie was out with Charles," their father announced without looking up from his paper. "She didn't get home until late."

Steffie feverishly worked the knife back and forth across the muffin, spreading the already thin layer of jam even thinner.

"Charles Tomaselli?" Norah repeated as though she wasn't sure she'd heard correctly.

"Two girls and a boy," David returned cheerfully.

"I beg your pardon?" Steffie asked.

"You and Charles," he answered. "You're going to be married and within the next few years have your own sweet family."

Rather than argue with her father or listen to more of this, Steffie glanced at her sister. "I need to do a few errands around town, but then I'm driving to Portland. Does anyone need anything?"

"Portland?" her father echoed. "Whatever for?"

"I thought it was time I applied for my doctorate and a part-time teaching position at the university. I *am* qualified, Dad, as well you know since you paid dearly for my education."

"But you can't worry about finding work now."

"I realize the country's in a recession, but—"

"I'm not talking about the economy," he muttered. "You're going to be married before the end of the summer, so don't go complicating everything with a job."

Steffie could feel the heat leap into her face. He seemed so sure of a marriage between her and Charles, and that exasperated her no end. "Dad, please listen—"

"It doesn't make sense for you to be starting a job or a course and then immediately taking time off for a honeymoon."

Steffie wasn't sure if it was a good idea to humor him any more. This had gone on long enough, but she didn't know what to say to him. Steffie was aware that her father claimed everything would work out between Valerie and Colby, too. After seeing her older sister's pale, drawn features that morning, Steffie had no faith in her father's words. Not that she'd really ever believed him . . .

"I don't actually expect to make a lot of contacts, since most of the offices won't be open on a Saturday, but I'm hoping to look around, check out the library, get a few names. Obtaining a teaching position now might be difficult, anyway, especially for the fall session. But I'd like to get started on a thesis soon."

"In other words you're going to Portland, no matter what I say?"

"Exactly."

"Shop when you're finished, then," her father suggested. "Try on a few wedding dresses. Both you and your sister are going to need one. Soon."

Norah was watching Steffie closely and spoke the moment their father had left the kitchen.

"What are we going to do?" Norah pleaded.

"I don't have a clue," Steffie said, fully agreeing with her sister's concern. "If Dad insists on believing—"

"Not Dad," Norah blurted out impatiently. "I'm talking about Valerie."

Steffie's exasperation with her father was quelled by her compassion for Valerie. "What can we do?"

Norah's face was pinched with worry. "That's the entire problem. I don't know, but we can't let her leave town like this. She came down early this morning.... I decided I had to tell her about Colby dating Sherry Waterman."

"How'd Valerie take it?"

"I don't know. She's so hard to read sometimes. It was as if she already knew, which I know is impossible." Norah frowned. "I wish you'd talk to her. She's in her room now and, Steffie, I'm really worried about her. She's in love with Colby—she admitted it—but she seems resigned to losing him."

Steffie thought she understood her older sister's feelings.

"To complicate matters," Norah continued, "Valerie and I started talking and ... arguing, and Dad heard us. He wanted to know what we were fighting about.''

''What did you say to him?''

''I didn't get a chance to say anything. Dad did all the talking. At least he and I agree. Dad believes Valerie should go talk this out with Colby, too. But I don't think she will.''

''Where's Valerie now?'' Steffie asked.

Norah looked away. ''She's upstairs.''

''Doing what?'' Her sister had been spending a lot of time alone in her room lately.

''I don't know, but I think you should go to her. Someone's got to. Valerie needs us, only she's so independent she doesn't know how to ask.''

Steffie disagreed. Her sister was getting—and apparently ignoring—advice from just about everyone, when what she needed to do was listen to her own heart.

''What's all this about you and Charles?'' Norah asked with open curiosity. ''I didn't know you even liked him.''

In light of their recent confrontation over the newspaper article, it was natural for her sister to assume that.

''We're just friends.''

''Which is definitely an improvement,'' Norah muttered.

Eager to leave before Norah asked more questions, Steffie went upstairs to her room. She toyed with the idea of talking to her sister, of telling her that seeking a long-distance cure for a broken heart didn't work.

But Valerie was intelligent enough to make her own decisions, and Steffie didn't feel qualified to say or do any more than she already had.

She dressed in a bright blue suit for her trip to Portland, one Valerie would have approved of had she been home. Her sister had mysteriously disappeared without saying where she was headed.

Steffie was on her way out the door when her father stopped her. "Sit on the porch with me a while, will you, Princess?"

"Of course." The wicker chair beside her father had belonged to her mother. Steffie sat next to him and gazed out over the sun-bright orchard she loved so dearly.

"Are you serious about this—getting a teaching position and all?"

"Yes. I can't stay home and do nothing. It'd be a terrible waste of my education."

"Wait, Princess."

All his talk of marriage was beginning to annoy her. "But, Dad—"

"Just for a couple of weeks. You've been home so short a while— I don't want you to move away just yet. All I ask is that you delay a bit longer."

"I won't be moving out right away..." She hesitated. She couldn't deny her father anything, and he knew it. "Two weeks," she promised reluctantly. "We'll visit, catch up, make some plans. Then I'll start looking for an apartment."

"Is Charles coming for dinner tonight?"

"No." She'd invited him, but he had a late-afternoon meeting and doubted he'd be back in time.

"He's going to miss out on your Italian dinner."

"There'll be others."

"You should fix a plate and take it into town for him. A bachelor like Charles doesn't often get the opportunity to enjoy a home-cooked dinner."

"He seems to be doing just fine on his own," Steffie said, hiding a smile. Her father wasn't even trying to be subtle.

"He's a fine young man."

"Yes, I know. I think he's probably one of the most talented newsmen I've ever read. To be honest, I'm surprised he's still in Orchard Valley. I thought one of the big-city newspapers would have lured him away long before now."

"They've tried, but Charles likes living here. He's turned down a number of job offers."

"How do you know?" That he'd received other offers didn't surprise Steffie, but that her father was privy to the information did. Then she remembered he and Charles had worked together on the farm-worker article.

"I know Charles quite well," her father answered. "We've become good friends the past few years."

Steffie crossed her legs. "I'd forgotten the two of you wrote that article."

Her father shook his head. "Charles wrote nearly every word of that story. All I did was get a few of the details for him and add a comment now and again, but that was it."

"He credits you with doing a lot more."

Her father was silent for a few moments, reflective. Steffie wondered if he was worrying about Valerie the way Norah had been. She was about to say something when her father spoke.

"Charles is going to make me a fine son-in-law."

Steffie closed her eyes, trying to control the burst of impatience his words produced.

"Daddy, don't, please," she murmured.

"Don't what?"

"Talk about Charles marrying me."

"Whyever not?" he asked, sounding almost offended. "Why, Princess, he's loved you for years, only I was too blind to notice. I guess I had my head in the clouds, because it's as clear as rainwater to me now. Soon after you left for Italy, he started coming around, asking about you. Only...that little devil...he was so subtle about it I didn't realize what he was doing until I saw the two of you together last night."

"I know, but—"

"You don't have a clue, do you?" her father said, chuckling and shaking his head. "Can't say I blame you since I didn't guess it myself."

The way her father made it sound, Charles had spent the past three years pining away for her. Steffie knew that couldn't be true. He was the reason she'd left. He'd humiliated her, laughed at her.

"When your mother mentioned you'd be marrying Charles—"

"Dad, *please.*" Steffie felt close to tears. "I'm not marrying Charles."

He studied her, eyes narrowed in concern. "What's wrong, Princess? You love him, don't you?"

"I did . . . but that was a long time ago when I was young and very foolish." Her father had no way of knowing just *how* foolish she'd been.

Even after the incident in Charles's home, when she'd soaked in his tub until her skin resembled that of a raisin, she hadn't stopped. Some odd quirk of her nature refused to let her believe he didn't want her, not when she loved him so desperately.

Oh, no, she hadn't been willing to leave well enough alone. So she'd plotted and planned his downfall.

Literally.

Leaving a message at the newspaper office that her father needed to see him right away, Steffie had waited in the stable for Charles's arrival. She'd spread fresh hay in the first stall.

No one was home and she tacked a note on the front door directing Charles to the stable.

He'd arrived right on time. She had to say that for him—he was punctual to a fault. He hesitated when he saw she was there alone, then asked to talk to her father. He kept his distance—which might have had something to do with the pitchfork in her hand.

Steffie had planned this meeting right down to the minutest detail. She'd worn tight jeans and a checkered shirt, half unbuttoned and tied at her waist.

She remembered Charles's repeating that he was anxious to talk to her father. Among other things, he'd told her, he wanted to clear the air about what was happening between him and Steffie.

At the time she'd nearly laughed out loud. Nothing was happening, despite her best efforts.

Steffie remembered again how perfect her timing had been. As she was chatting with him, explaining that she wasn't sure where her father had gone, she set aside the pitchfork and started up the ladder that led to the loft. At precisely the right moment, she lost her balance, just as she'd planned. After teetering for a second, she dropped into Charles's arms.

He broke her fall, but the impact of her weight slamming against him had taken them both to the floor, and into the fresh hay. For a moment, neither said a word.

"Are you all right?" He spoke first, his voice low and angry.

Steffie had never been more "all right" in her life. For the first time she was in Charles's arms and he held on to her as though he never intended to let her go, as though this was exactly where he'd always wanted her to be.

Steffie had gazed down on him and slowly shaken her head. His gaze had gone to her softly parted lips and then his hands were in her hair and with a groan he'd guided her mouth to his. The kiss was wild, crazily intense. No man had ever kissed her with such hunger or need. Steffie didn't understand what she was feeling; all she knew was that she wanted Charles more than she'd ever wanted anything.

While his kisses had been frenzied, his touch was gentle. His hands had cupped her breasts and she must have gasped with surprise and delight because he abruptly jerked away.

She had protested, wanting him to touch her, begging him. The sheer excitement of what she'd experienced had taken her by force. Not knowing how to tell him, she'd done what came instinctively. She'd kissed him back with the same searing hunger, until it seemed neither of them would be able to endure the intensity of their lovemaking any longer.

Steffie would never forget the way he'd rolled away from her, bounding effortlessly to his feet, breathing hard.

At first he'd said nothing. Steffie knew she'd have to speak first. So she'd looked up at him and said what had been on her heart from the moment they first met. She'd told him simply, honestly, how much she loved him.

Steffie would forever remember what happened next.

Charles had stared down at her in silence for several heart-stopping seconds, and then he'd begun to laugh. Deep belly laughs, as though she'd said the funniest thing he'd ever heard.

She was exactly what he needed, he'd said with a twist of sarcasm, a lovesick teenager following him around like a motherless calf. How many times did he have to tell her he wasn't interested? When he was ready for a woman in his life, he wanted exactly that, a *woman*, not a child. Especially not one as immature as she was.

He'd said more, but by then Steffie was running toward the house, tears streaking her face. The sound of his laughter had followed her, taunting her, ridiculing her.

"Charles has loved you all these years," her father said now. He spoke confidently, crashing into her memories and dragging her back to the present. The past was so painful that Steffie was content to leave it behind.

"He's never loved me," she whispered through a haze of remembered pain.

"Ah, my sweet Princess," her father countered. "That's where you're wrong."

CHAPTER SIX

"DAD, LISTEN TO ME." Steffie stood abruptly and thrust her head away for fear her father would see the tears glistening in her eyes. "Whatever you do, please don't say anything to Charles about—you know?"

"Being in love with you?"

"That, too," she pleaded, "but I'm particularly concerned about this marriage thing."

"That troubles you?"

"Yes, Dad, it troubles me a great deal."

"You don't understand, do you?" he asked softly.

"Oh, Dad, you're the one who doesn't understand."

"Steffie, my Princess, don't limit yourself to the things you understand," her father said in the gentlest voice imaginable, "otherwise you'll miss half of what life has to offer."

She had to leave, had to escape before she dissolved into an emotional storm of tears. Not until she was in the car, heading she didn't know where, did she realize her father hadn't promised one way or the other. He might well blurt out everything to Charles.

By the time Steffie had reached Orchard Valley, she'd composed herself. She'd do her errands—pick up dry cleaning, visit the small local library, mail a birthday card to little Mario in Italy—before she drove to Portland. Because it was Saturday, Main Street was busy and she was fortunate to find a parking spot. Not so fortunate as she would have liked, however, since the only available space was directly in front of the newspaper office.

For at least ten minutes, Steffie sat in the family station wagon, considering whether to talk to Charles herself. *Should* she warn him about her father's crazy dream, his matchmaking hopes?

She was still debating the issue when she saw him, talking to the girl at the front desk. Her heart gladdened at the mere sight of him. He'd removed his suit jacket and the sleeves of his white shirt were rolled halfway up his arms. He was so attractive, so compelling. For several moments she watched him, mesmerized, and her heart beat faster.

At first glance, Steffie thought Charles might have been talking to Norah, but she quickly realized that was impossible. The resemblance was there, though. This girl was blond and exceptionally pretty. Even from inside her car, Steffie could see how she gazed up at Charles with wide, adoring eyes.

The dread that went through her was immediate and unstoppable. She was jealous, and she hated it. The blonde was probably Wendy, the apprentice Charles had mentioned, and Steffie didn't doubt for an instant that she was in love with him. Not that Steffie blamed her; she'd once played the role of doting female herself. Was playing it even now, despite her most strenuous efforts.

Charles was still talking to his apprentice, his hand resting against the back of her chair. He leaned forward as the two of them reviewed something, their heads close together. The blonde laughed at some remark of his and smiled up at him, her heart in her eyes.

Steffie couldn't watch any more. It was like looking back three years and seeing what a fool she'd made of herself. Hurriedly she got out of the car and swung her purse over her shoulder. Forcing her eyes away from the newspaper office, she locked the car door. She was about to move away when Charles stepped onto the sidewalk.

"Stephanie, hello." He sounded surprised to see her. More than that, he sounded pleased.

"Hi," she returned awkwardly, feeling guilty, though she wasn't sure why. It wasn't as if she'd actually been spying on him.

"Where are you headed?" he asked, giving her business suit an appreciative glance.

"I—I was thinking about driving into Portland and visiting the university, after I do some errands here. I plan eventually to rent an apartment of my own in the city, but Dad . . ." She hesitated.

Charles grinned knowingly. "But your father wasn't delighted with the idea."

"Exactly. I promised him I'd wait another couple of weeks."

"Why two weeks?"

"Uh..." For a few seconds, she panicked, wondering if Charles had guessed, wondering if her father had mentioned his dream, praying he hadn't. "You'll have to ask him."

"Have you got a moment? I'd like you to meet Wendy. She's the apprentice I was telling you about. Bart's here, as well. You remember Bart, don't you?"

Steffie bit her lip, feeling reluctant. The last time she'd been to the newspaper office she'd come bent on vengeance, with threats of a lawsuit burning in her eyes.

"I'll tell you what, I'll throw in lunch. I've got an appointment at one, but we have plenty of time."

She was still caught in the throes of indecision, when Charles took her firmly by the elbow and escorted her inside. She felt a wave of relief; after all, the opportunity to spend time with him, even a few minutes squeezed in between appointments, was too precious to decline.

It might have been Steffie's imagination, but the people in the newspaper office seemed delighted to see her. She wondered what Charles could possibly have said to salvage her reputation.

A couple of the reporters, one of whom she remembered from high school, welcomed her back to Orchard Valley. Bart, the pressman, inquired about her father's health. Even Wendy seemed inclined to like her, which raised Steffie's guilt by several uncomfortable notches.

"I'll be back at one," Charles said as he guided Steffie out the front door.

"But—" Bart stopped abruptly when Charles cut him off with a glare.

"I'll be here in plenty of time," he promised. "What's your pleasure?" he asked, smiling down at her.

"Whatever's most convenient for you."

"The Half Moon's serving sandwiches now. How does that sound?"

"Great." When Steffie left for Italy, the Half Moon, just down the street from the *Clarion*, had been a small coffee shop.

Now she saw that it had been expanded and modernized. While Charles placed their order, Steffie found them a table. Several customers, old acquaintances, greeted her and asked about her father, and before she realized it, she was completely at ease, laughing and joking with the people around her.

When Charles returned with their turkey-and-tomato sandwiches and coffee, she smiled at him happily, content to shed the troubled thoughts she'd carried into town with her. At least for the moment...

"How's your father this morning?" Charles asked, holding his sandwich with both hands to keep bits of tomato and lettuce from escaping.

"Cantankerous as ever." Opinionated, too, and occasionally illogical, but she didn't mention any of that. Even if she decided to warn Charles, now didn't seem to be the time. Not when they were sitting across from each other, relaxed and light-hearted, and all the world felt right.

The hour passed quickly. This kind of pure, simple happiness never lasted, she told herself. But, oh, how she wished it could. Charles seemed equally reluctant for their time to end.

Steffie walked back to work with him. "Thanks for lunch," she said, standing on the sidewalk in front of the office.

"I'll call you," Charles promised as Bart came out of the office, glancing anxiously at his watch. "All right, all right," Charles told him impatiently. He turned back to Steffie. "Sometime tomorrow?"

"Sure." She nodded eagerly.

Sometime tomorrow. A few, short hours and yet it felt like a lifetime away.

VALERIE WAS LEAVING.

Steffie did try talking to her. She'd tried to explain that running away from love wouldn't help; it would just follow her wherever she went. Her sister had listened, then quietly packed her bags.

Sunday morning, when Valerie was about to depart, Colby showed up unexpectedly. Steffie didn't think she'd ever been more excited. It was as if everything she'd read about the power of love, everything she'd always secretly believed, was true. Colby would prove it. He'd come to declare his love and sweep Valerie off her feet.

It soon became clear, however, that Colby wasn't there because of Valerie. He hadn't realized she was catching a flight that afternoon, and when he was told, he seemed to accept it as inevitable. Furthermore, he had no intention of stopping her. No intention of asking her to stay. If anything, he seemed almost relieved at her imminent departure.

When the moment came for Valerie to go, Steffie thought she might burst into tears herself. She'd so desperately wanted to believe in the power of love, in its ability to knock down barriers and leap over obstacles.

Valerie had hugged them all farewell, and with shoulders held stiff and straight, walked from the porch to her rental car. Then, just before she left, she'd turned and looked at Colby.

Steffie would always remember the tenderness she saw in her sister's eyes. It was as though she'd reached back, one last time, to say goodbye... and to thank him. At least, that was how it seemed to Steffie. She'd never been so affected by a mere glance. That look of Valerie's was full of love, but it also expressed dignity and a gracious acceptance.

Steffie was left to sort out her mingled emotions of anger and pain as Valerie drove away. She turned to Colby, who still stared after her sister's car. It took every ounce of self-control she possessed not to scream at him. Only the anguish in his eyes prevented her from lashing out, and when she recognized the intensity of his pain, her own anger was replaced by a bleak hopelessness.

"She's gone," he whispered.

"She'll be back," her father said with the same unquestioning confidence that had driven Steffie nearly mad with frustration.

"No," she answered, her voice quavering. "She won't. Not for a very long time."

She couldn't refrain from voicing a few other hard truths. Then, unable to face either Colby or her father any longer, she dashed back into the house. Norah followed soon afterward, and Steffie realized that her younger sister was crying.

"She's going to marry Rowdy Cassidy," Norah wailed. "What's so terrible is that she doesn't even *love* him."

"Then what makes you think Valerie would do anything so foolish?" Steffie asked calmly. Valerie might be unhappy about losing Colby Winston, but she was too sensible to enter into a loveless marriage.

"You don't understand," Norah said as she continued to sob. "*He's* in love with her. He's called nearly every day and sent flowers and . . . and Valerie's so vulnerable right now. I just know she's going to make a terrible mistake."

"Val's not going to do anything stupid," Steffie reassured her sister. Valerie wouldn't marry her boss on the rebound—Steffie was confident of that. Deep down, she knew exactly what her sister would be doing for the next three years—if not longer. She knew because she'd done it herself. Valerie would try to escape into her work, to the exclusion of everything else. Because then she wouldn't have time to hurt, time to deal with regrets and might-have-beens. She wouldn't have time to look back or relive the memories.

An hour later, Steffie took a glass of iced tea out to her father, who stubbornly refused to leave the porch.

He sat in his rocking chair, anxiously studying the road. "They'll both be back," he said again.

Steffie didn't try to disillusion him. By nightfall he'd be forced to accept the truth without her prompting.

Within ten minutes of Valerie's departure, Colby had left, too. He hadn't raced down the driveway in hot pursuit or given the slightest indication that he was going anywhere but back to town.

"Mark my words," her father said confidently. "Valerie and Colby will be married before the end of June."

"Dad..."

"And you and Charles will follow a few weeks later. All three of my daughters are going to marry this summer. I know it in my heart, as surely as I know my name."

Although she nearly choked on it, Steffie swallowed her words of argument.

Needing some physical activity to vent her frustrations, she saddled Princess. She knew better than to try her luck with Fury again. But the mare, who was generally docile, seemed to sense Steffie's mood and galloped like the wind down the long pasture road and then across the rocky field until they reached the bluff. The same place Fury had taken her.

Holding the reins, Steffie slid off the mare's back and sat on the very rock she had before. She lost track of time as she sat looking out on the valley, thinking about Valerie. And Colby. Remembering her own disastrous relationship with Charles, and how her willful behavior had destroyed any chance they'd had three years ago. Now there seemed to be a fresh beginning for her and Charles, however fragile it might be. Not for Valerie, though... Life wasn't fair, she thought, and love doesn't make everything perfect.

She rode slowly back and had just finished rubbing down Princess and leading her into her stall when Charles appeared. "I thought I heard someone back here." He stood by the stable door, hands on his hips, smiling.

"Charles." She shouldn't have been so surprised to see him. After all, he'd made a point of telling her that he'd be in touch.

"Your dad thought you'd gone out riding, but seemed to think you'd be home soon."

"Have you been waiting long?"

"Not really. Your father's kept me entertained."

"Is he still on the front porch?"

"He hasn't moved since I got here."

Dispirited, Steffie looked away. "That's what I was afraid of. Valerie's gone, and he seems to believe she'll come back if he sits there long enough."

Charles frowned heavily. "Is something going on? A problem?"

"No," she answered quickly, perhaps too quickly because Charles's eyes narrowed suspiciously. "I mean, nothing you need to worry about. Dad desperately wants to believe Colby and Val will kiss and make up—that's the reason he's being so stubborn. By dinnertime he'll be forced to recognize that it simply isn't going to happen."

It might have been because she was nervous and flustered, or maybe she just wasn't watching where she was going, but Steffie tripped over a bale of hay.

Although she threw out her arms in an effort to right herself, it was too late. She fell forward, but before she completely lost her balance, Charles caught her around the waist. He twisted his body so that when they went down, he took the brunt of the fall.

It was as though three years had evaporated. They'd been in virtually the same position then, with Steffie sprawled over him, her heart pounding. Only this time she hadn't manipulated the circumstances. This time she wasn't in control.

They were both breathing hard. A tumult of confused emotions raged within her, and she braced her arms against him, ready to get up quickly and move away. Instead, his arms, which were around her waist, held her firmly in place.

"It seems we've been here before," he said, his eyes gazing into hers.

"I—" She stopped abruptly and nodded.

"Do you remember what happened that day?"

Incapable of speaking, she nodded again.

"Do you remember the way we kissed?"

She couldn't look at him, couldn't allow him to read the answer in her eyes. "Let me go," she pleaded, her voice weak, her eyes tightly shut.

"Not yet."

She struggled, but he held her fast for another long moment before he gradually eased his hold. "Let's talk about that time."

"No," she cried. The instant she was free, she rushed to her feet, not realizing she must have sprained her ankle. But when she placed her weight on her left foot she experienced a sharp stabbing pain. She couldn't suppress a whimper as she leaned against the stall door for support.

"You're hurt," Charles said, immediately getting to his feet. He slipped his arm around her waist.

"I'm sure it's nothing. I've just twisted my ankle—it hardly hurts at all," she lied.

Without another word, Charles effortlessly scooped her up into his arms.

"Charles, please," she said, growing angry. "I'm perfectly fine. It's a minor sprain, nothing more. There's no need for this."

He didn't reply but began to carry her out of the stable.

"Where are you taking me?" she demanded.

"The kitchen. You should put ice on it right away."

"I want you to know I don't appreciate these cave-man tactics."

"That's too bad." He was short of breath by the time he reached the back door, which infuriated Steffie even more. "Put me down this instant," she snapped.

"In a minute." He managed, after some difficulty, to open the door, then deposited her unceremoni-ously in a chair—like a sack of flour, she thought with irritation. He was pulling open the freezer section of the refrigerator and removing the ice-cube tray.

She rested her sore foot on her opposite knee and was about to remove her shoe when he stopped her. "I'll do that."

"Charles, you're being ridiculous."

He didn't answer, but carefully drew off her shoe and sock. His fingers were tender as he examined her ankle, and it felt strangely intimate to have him touch her like this.

"I told you already—it doesn't hurt anymore," she argued. "I might have gotten up too fast or put my foot down wrong. I don't feel a thing now."

"Try standing up."

Cautiously, she did. His arm circled her waist as she gingerly placed her weight on the foot. "See," she said, feeling both triumphant and foolish. "There doesn't seem to be any damage."

"I wouldn't be so sure. Try walking."

The floor felt cool against her bare foot. She took a guarded first step, biting her lower lip. There was hardly a twinge. She tried again. Same result. "See?" she said. "I'm fine." And she proceeded to prove it by marching around the kitchen.

"Good." Charles replaced the ice-cube tray in the freezer, but he was frowning.

"Don't look so disappointed," she teased as she pulled on her sock and shoe.

He glanced at her, then smiled slowly, sensually. "I've heard of some inventive ways to avoiding kissing a man, but..." He let the rest fade as he sat down beside her, then pulled her chair toward him until they sat face-to-face, so close that their knees touched.

Steffie closed her eyes as his hands came to rest on her shoulders. His breathing grew ragged and he whispered her name. "Stephanie," he called her, leaning forward to touch her lips with his own.

Steffie was afraid—of his kiss and of her own response. But she felt a thrill of excitement, too. He must have sensed that, because the quality of his kiss changed from gentle caress to fierce possession.

Charles groaned, and she trembled at the sound of his desire for her. She slid her hands up his chest, delighting in the feel of hard, smooth muscles as she gave herself fully to his kiss.

Abruptly he broke away, his shoulders heaving with the effort. Caught by surprise, Steffie let her eyes flutter open and for a long silent moment they stared at each other, her breath wheezing through lips that were moist and swollen.

His hand reached out to touch her hair, a small, intimate gesture that moved her unbearably.

Then he stretched out his arms, gripping her by the waist and lifting her from the chair to set her securely in his lap. She wasn't given the opportunity to protest before his mouth claimed hers once more.

This time his kiss was slow and gentle, as tender as the earlier kiss had been hungry and demanding. She felt herself melting in his arms, surrendering the last of her resistance.

"I want to talk about what happened," he whispered.

She knew what he meant, and she wanted none of it. The scene in the stable was much too painful to examine even now. "That was in the past."

"It has to be settled between us."

"No," she argued, trying to change his mind with a deep, hungry kiss.

His voice was whiskey-rough when she finished. "Steff, we have to clear the past before we can talk about the future."

"We only just met, remember?" He was the one who'd suggested they start over again. He couldn't bury the past and then ask that they exhume it.

"Just listen to me..."

"Not yet," she pleaded. Maybe never, her heart insisted, balking at the idea of reliving a time that had been so painful for her.

"Soon." He tangled his fingers in her hair and spread kisses across her face.

"Maybe," she agreed reluctantly.

The sound of laughter broke into the haze of her pleasure. At least Steffie assumed it was laughter. It took her a wild moment to realize the sound was coming from the porch, and that it must be her father. Not knowing what to think, she slowly broke away from Charles.

"Is that David laughing?" he asked.

Steffie shrugged. "I'd better find out if something's wrong."

He nodded, and they walked hand in hand to the porch.

"Dad?" she asked softly when she reached her father, rocking contentedly on the porch. His smile broadened when he saw her and Charles. His gaze fell to their hands, which were still clasped tightly together, and his eyes fairly twinkled. "Check the freezer, will you? By heaven, I wish I'd thought of this sooner."

"The freezer?" she repeated, glancing at Charles, wondering if her father had lost his wits. "Why do you want me to check it?"

"We need something special to fix for dinner tonight. We're going to have a celebration!"

Steffie frowned in puzzlement. "What kind of celebration?"

"There's going to be a wedding in the family."

Steffie groaned inwardly. "Dad..."

"Don't argue with me, Princess, there isn't time."

"But, Dad..."

"See there?" he said, pointing toward the long stretch of driveway. "What did I tell you?"

Steffie looked, but she couldn't see anything except a small puff of dust, barely discernible against the skyline.

"I was about to give up on those two," he said with a wry chuckle. "They're both too stubborn for their own good. I have to admit they gave me pause, but your mother was right. Guess I should have known better than to doubt her."

"Dad, what in heaven's name are you talking about?"

"Your sister and Colby. They're on their way back to the house now."

Steffie glanced up again, and this time the make and color of the car was unmistakable. Colby was returning to the house. And although she couldn't clearly tell who the passenger was, she almost knew it had to be her sister.

CHAPTER SEVEN

"EVEN NOW I can't believe it," Valerie said wistfully, sitting cross-legged on her bed. Steffie and Norah lounged on the opposite end, listening.

"Colby actually chased you down on the freeway?" Norah wanted to know.

Valerie's smile lit up her whole face as she nodded. "It really was romantic to have him race after me. He told me he didn't realize he was planning to do it until he was on the interstate."

"You've got everything worked out?" Steffie asked. From what Norah had told her, and from remarks Valerie herself had made, she knew there were a lot of obstacles standing in the way of this marriage.

"We've talked things out the best we can. It's been a struggle to find the right compromises. I've got a call in to Rowdy Cassidy at CHIPS. I think I can talk him into letting me open a branch of the company in Oregon. He's already done a feasibility study for the Pacific Northwest. He was just waiting until he could find the right person to head it up. He didn't originally have me in mind, but I don't think he'll have a problem giving it to me. Then again—" she paused thoughtfully "—it may be better to discuss this in person."

"Colby doesn't mind if you continue working?" Norah's voice was tinged with disbelief.

"No. Because it's what I need. Naturally he'd rather I was there to pamper him when he gets home from the hospital every night, but this way we'll learn to pamper each other."

"I'm so happy for you." Steffie leaned forward to hug her sister. Valerie's eyes reflected an inner joy that Steffie had never seen in her before. This was what love—real love—did for a person. When two people cared this deeply for each other, it couldn't help but show.

"Now that we've decided to go ahead with the wedding, Colby wants to arrange it as soon as possible," Valerie went on to say. "I hope everyone's willing to work fast and hard because we've got a wedding to plan for next month."

"Next month!" Norah's blue eyes rounded incredulously.

"I was lucky to get him to wait that long. Colby would rather we flew to Vegas tonight and were done with it."

"No way" was Norah and Steffie's automatic response.

"I never thought I'd be the sentimental sort," Valerie admitted sheepishly, "but I realized I want a large fancy wedding. Colby loves me enough to agree to one, as long as I organize it quickly. Once that man makes a decision, there's no holding him back."

Steffie smiled to herself. Dr. Colby Winston was in for a real surprise. Valerie was talented enough in the organizational department to manage the United Nations. If he gave her a month to arrange their wedding, she'd do a beautiful job of it with time to spare.

A wedding so soon meant the family was about to be caught up in a whirlwind of activity, but that suited Steffie. It was time for them to celebrate. The grieving, the anxiety, were over.

"You've been seeing a lot of Charles lately, haven't you?" Norah asked, looking expectantly at Steffie. "Do you think we could make this a double wedding?"

Valerie smiled broadly at Steffie, as though she'd be in favor of the idea, too.

"I haven't been seeing *that* much of Charles," Steffie answered, thrusting out her chin. She realized she sounded defensive. "Well, I—I suppose we have been together quite a bit lately, but there's certainly never been any talk of marriage."

"I've always liked Charles," Norah said, studying Steffie closely. "I mean, I could go for this guy, given the least bit of encouragement. First Valerie falls in love and now you. You know, it's a little unfair. I'm the one who lives at home and you two fly in and within a couple of weeks nab the two most eligible men in town."

"Me?" Steffie argued. "You make it sound like a done deal. Trust me, it isn't."

"You're in love with him," Valerie said quietly.

Steffie didn't reply. She was unwilling to openly admit her feelings for Charles. It would be so easy to fool herself into believing he did hold some tenderness for her. But he'd never said so, and other than a few shared kisses he hadn't given her any indication he cared.

But he had, something inside her said.

Steffie refused to listen. She couldn't, wouldn't, forget that she'd made a fool of herself over him, not once but three times. Because she'd cared, and he hadn't.

"I don't know how Charles feels about me," Steffie said in a soft steady voice.

"You're joking!" Norah exclaimed.

And Valerie added, "Steffie, it's obvious how he feels."

Steffie discounted their assurances with a shrug. "For all I know, he could be hanging around me in order to get close to Norah."

"Charles? No way." Both Valerie and Norah burst into loud peals of laughter.

"Are you saying you wouldn't mind me dating him?" Norah teased, winking at Valerie.

"Feel free." In fact, Steffie would throttle Norah if she went within ten feet of Charles, though she could hardly say so.

"I hope you're joking," Norah said, shaking her head. "I should have realized what was going on a long time ago. I don't know how I could've been so dense. Charles and Dad became friends shortly after you left—good friends."

"That doesn't prove a thing," Steffie insisted. She didn't need anyone else building up her hopes, and although her sisters meant well, their encouragement would only make her disappointment harder to bear.

"It wouldn't mean much if Charles hadn't made a point of asking about you every time he stopped by," Norah was saying. "I have to hand it to the guy, though—he was always subtle about his questions."

"Now that you mention it, whenever I talked to Charles, Steffie's name cropped up in the conversation," Valerie reported thoughtfully. "I should have guessed myself."

"You were too involved with Colby to see anything else," Norah teased and then sighed. She crossed her arms and rested them atop her bent knees. "Don't get me wrong, I'm happy for you two, but I wish I'd fall in love. Don't you think it's my turn?"

"Aren't you leaping to conclusions here?" Steffie asked. She wasn't exactly sporting an engagement ring the way Valerie was. She and Charles hadn't arrived at that stage of commitment—and probably never would. Besides, her mistakes with him three years ago had been the result of leaping to certain incorrect conclusions about his feelings, and she wasn't ready for a repeat performance.

STEFFIE DIDN'T SEE Charles again until Tuesday afternoon. She wasn't surprised not to hear from him, knowing how involved he was with the production of the newspaper during the first part of every week.

Valerie and Steffie had driven into town to visit The Petal Pusher, the local flower shop. Valerie had decided on a spring color theme for her wedding and had already chosen material for Steffie's and Norah's gowns in a pale shade of green and a delicate rose.

Valerie angled the car into the slot closest to the flower shop. Since the newspaper office was almost directly across the street, it was natural for her to glance curiously in that direction.

"You haven't talked to Charles in a couple of days, have you?"

"He's busy with the paper."

"There's time to stop in now and say hello if you want. I'll be talking to the florist, so you might as well."

Steffie was tempted, but felt uncomfortable about interrupting Charles at work. "Some other time," she said with a feigned lack of interest, though in actuality she was starving for the sight of him. Helping Valerie plan her wedding had forced some long-buried emotions to the surface. Steffie hadn't admitted until these past few weeks how deeply she longed for marriage herself. A family of her own. A husband to love and live with her whole life.

A husband.

Her mind stumbled over the word. There'd only ever been one man she could imagine as her husband, and that was Charles. Even though Steffie knew it was unwise, she'd started dreaming again. She found herself fantasizing what her life would be like if she was married ... to Charles. She wanted to blame her sisters for putting such thoughts in her head, but she couldn't. Those dreams and fantasies had been there for years now. The problem was that she couldn't suppress them anymore.

An hour later at the same moment as Steffie and Valerie were leaving the flower shop, Charles happened to walk out of the *Clarion* office.

Steffie instinctively looked across the street, where he was walking with Wendy, deeply involved in conversation. Something must have told him she was there because he glanced in her direction. He grinned warmly.

Steffie relaxed and waved. He returned the gesture, then spoke to Wendy before jogging across the street to join Steffie and her sister.

"Hello," he said, but his gaze lingered on Steffie. He barely seemed to notice Valerie's presence.

"Hi." It was ridiculous to feel so shy with him. "I'd have stopped in to say hello, but I knew you'd be busy."

"I'm never too busy for you." His eyes were affectionate and welcoming.

"See," Valerie hissed close to Steffie's ear. Then, more loudly, "I've got a couple of errands to run, if you two would like a chance to talk."

Charles checked his watch. "Come back to the office with me?"

"Sure." If he'd suggested they stand on their heads in the middle of Main Street, Steffie would have willingly agreed. Fool that she was!

Valerie cast a quick glance at the clock tower. "How about if I meet you back at the car in—"

"Half an hour," Charles supplied, reaching for Steffie's hand. "There's something I'd like to show you," he told her.

"Fine, I'll see you then, Steff," Valerie returned cheerfully. She set off at a brisk walk, without looking back.

Their fingers entwined, Charles led Steffie across the street to the newspaper office. "I was going to save this for later, but now's as good a time as any." He ushered her in and guided her down the center aisle, past the obviously busy staff, to his desk.

Steffie wasn't sure what to expect, but a mock-up of the *Clarion*'s second page wasn't it. As far as she could see, it was the same as any other inside page that she'd read over the years.

"Clearly I'm missing something," she said after a moment. "Is the type different?"

"Nope, we've used the same printing fonts as always." He crossed his arms and leaned against the desk, looking exceptionally pleased with himself.

"How about a hint?" she asked, a bit puzzled.

"I might suggest you read the masthead," he said next, his dark eyes gleaming.

"The masthead," she repeated thoughtfully as she scanned the listings of the newspaper's personnel and the duties they performed

"All right, I will. Charles Tomaselli, editor and publisher. Roger Simons..."

"Stop right there," he said, holding up his hand.

"Publisher," she said again. "That's new. What exactly does it mean?"

His smile could have lit up a Christmas tree. "It means, my beautiful Stephanie, that I now own the *Orchard Valley Clarion.*"

"Charles, that's wonderful!" She resisted the urge to throw her arms around him, but it was difficult.

"My dream's got a mortgage attached," he told her wryly. "A lot of folks think I'm a fool to risk so much of my future on an informational medium that's said to be dying. Newspapers are folding all over the country."

"The *Clarion* won't."

"Not as long as I can help it."

Her heart seemed to be spilling over with joy. She knew how much Charles loved his work, how committed he was to the community. "I'm so excited about this."

"Me too," he admitted, his smile boyishly proud. "I'd say this calls for a celebration, wouldn't you?"

"Most definitely."

"Dinner?"

She nodded eagerly and they set the date for Thursday evening, deciding on a restaurant that overlooked the Columbia River Gorge, about an hour's drive north.

Steffie felt as if her feet didn't touch the pavement as she hurried across the street thirty minutes later to meet her sister. Never, in all the time she'd known Charles, had she seen him happier. And she was happy with him, and for him. That was what loving someone meant. It was a truth she hadn't really understood before, not until today. This intense new feeling had taught her that real love wasn't prideful or selfish. Real love meant sharing the happiness—and the sorrows—of the person you loved. She understood that now. She realized that her past obsession with Charles had focused more on her own desires than on his. Her love had matured.

Charles had wakened within her emotions she hadn't known it was possible to experience. Emotions, and sensations. When she was with him, especially when he kissed her, she felt vibrant and alive.

"You look like you're about to cry, you're so happy," Valerie said when Steffie joined her in the car. "I don't suppose Charles popped the question."

"No," she said with a sigh. "But he asked me to dinner to help him celebrate. Guess what? Charles is the new owner of the *Clarion*."

Valerie didn't seem nearly as excited as Steffie. "He's going to be working a lot of extra hours then, isn't he?"

"He didn't say." If he spent as much time at the newspaper as he had three years earlier, there wouldn't be any extra hours left.

"I suppose his eating habits are atrocious."

Steffie suspected they were, but she shrugged. "I wouldn't know."

"I bet he enjoys a home-cooked meal every now and again, though, don't you?"

Steffie eyed her sister suspiciously. "Is there a point to this conversation?"

"Of course," she answered with a sly grin. "I think you should heat up some of that fabulous spaghetti sauce and take it to him later. You know what they say about the way to a man's heart, don't you?"

"Funny, that sounds exactly like a suggestion of Dad's. What's your interest in this?"

"Well," Valerie admitted coyly, "that way I wouldn't feel guilty about asking you if I could take some with me to Colby's. If he tasted your spaghetti sauce and happened to assume, through no error of mine, that I'd cooked up this fabulous dinner—" she paused to inhale deeply "—he'd be so overcome by the idea of marrying such a fabulous cook that he'd go over the wedding list with me and not put it off for the third time."

"There's method in your madness, Valerie Bloomfield."

"Naturally. Colby doesn't know that I can't tell one side of a cookie sheet from the other. I don't want to disillusion him quite so soon. He suggested I cook dinner tonight and, well, you get the picture."

"I do indeed. I'll be happy to share the spaghetti sauce with you."

"I'll hang around the kitchen to be sure some of the aroma sticks to me."

"I'll give you the recipe if you want."

"I want, but if I have trouble cooking with a microwave, heaven only knows what I'll do once I'm around a stove. One with burners and a real oven."

Steffie chuckled. She certainly had no objection to helping her sister prepare dinner for Colby, but she wasn't sure taking a plate over to Charles's house was such a good plan.

Valerie and Norah convinced her otherwise.

"Charles never did get to sample your cooking," Norah reminded her. "He stopped by and you offered him dinner, but he'd already eaten. Remember?"

"How'd you know that?"

Norah looked mildly surprised, as though everyone must be aware of what went on between Steffie and Charles. "Dad told me."

Her dear, matchmaking father. Steffie should have known.

"It isn't going to hurt anything," Valerie reminded her. "If you want, you can ride into town with me. I'll go over to Charles's house with you and we can drop off the meal."

Steffie still wasn't sure, but Norah and Valerie believed it was a romantic thing to do. They both seemed to think Charles was serious about their relationship.

As for Steffie, she didn't know what to think anymore. In fact she preferred not to think about their relationship at all. And yet...

She remained hesitant about this project of delivering him a surprise dinner but Valerie and Norah were so certain it would be a success that she went ahead with it.

They were apparently right.

Steffie was propped up in her bed reading a new mystery novel at ten-thirty that night. Her bedroom window was open and a breeze whispered softly through the orchard. The house was quiet; her father had gone to bed an hour earlier, and her sisters were both out for the evening.

When the phone chimed, she answered on the first ring, not wanting it to wake her father.

"How'd you do it?" Charles asked, sounding thoroughly delighted. "I came home exhausted and hungry, thinking I was going to have to throw something in the microwave for dinner. The minute I walked into the house, I smelled this heavenly scent of basil and garlic. I followed my nose to the table and found your note."

"You should thank Valerie and Norah. The whole thing was their idea." Had he been furious, Steffie would gladly have shifted the blame, so she figured it was only fair to share the credit.

"I haven't tasted spaghetti that good since my grandmother died. I'd forgotten how delicious home-made sauce can be."

Steffie was warmed by the compliment. "I'm glad you enjoyed it."

"Enjoyed it! You have no idea. It was like stepping back into my childhood to spend the evening with my grandmother. She was a fabulous cook, and so are you."

Steffie leaned against the heap of pillows and closed her eyes, savoring these precious moments.

"The bottle of wine and the small loaf of French bread were a nice touch," he told her, sounding pleased and more than a little tired.

"I'm glad," she said again. A dozen unnamed emotions whirled inside her.

"I wish you didn't live so far out of town," Charles said next. "Otherwise I'd come over right now—to thank you."

"I wish I didn't live so far out, too."

"Since we're both tossing out wishes, there are a few other things I'd like, as well," he added in tones as smooth as velvet.

"You're limited to three." How raspy her own voice sounded.

Charles chuckled softly. "Only three? What happens if I want four?"

"I'm not sure, but I seem to remember reading once about a handsome young newsman who was turned into a frog because he got greedy over wishes."

"How many have I got left?"

"Two."

"All right, I'll choose carefully. I wish we were together in your father's stable right now."

"You're wasting one of your wishes on the stable?"

"That's what I said. It seems as though every time I'm there, you end up in my arms. In fact, I'm looking forward to visiting your father's horses again soon."

"That can be easily arranged. Fury and Princess will be thrilled."

"I'm glad to hear it," he murmured. Steffie could picture him sprawled comfortably on his sofa, talking to her, a glass of wine in one hand.

"Be warned, you have only one wish left."

"Give me a moment—I want to make this one good. I've had two glasses of wine and in case you haven't noticed, I'm feeling kind of mellow."

"I noticed." She smiled to herself.

"Know what I'd like?"

"You tell me," she teased.

"With my last wish, I'd like to wipe out the past."

Steffie realized immediately that he was referring to their encounters three years ago. "That one's easy," she said, and even though he couldn't see her, she made a sweeping motion with her hand. "There. It's gone, forgotten, never to be discussed again."

"Uh-oh. I think I made a mistake."

"Why's that?"

"We can't sweep it away."

"Why not?" she asked, striving for a flippant air. "It was one of your wishes, and it's in my power to grant it and so I have."

"But I don't want it wiped out completely. Let's talk about it now, Stephanie, get it over with once and for all."

Steffie's heart jolted. "Sorry, it's gone, vanished. I haven't a clue what you're talking about." Willfully she lowered her voice, half pleading with him, not wanting anything to ruin these moments.

The silence stretched between them. "You're right, this isn't something we can discuss over the phone. Certainly not when I'm half drunk and you're so far away."

"You're tired."

"It's funny," Charles told her, and she could hear the satisfaction in his voice. "I'm so exhausted I'm dead on my feet, and at the same time I feel so elated I want to take you in my arms and whirl you around the room."

"You never once mentioned buying the paper." She didn't mean it as a criticism. But he'd managed to keep it a secret not only from her, but from just about everyone in town. When Steffie mentioned Charles's news to her father, he'd been as pleasantly surprised as she.

"I couldn't, but believe me, I was dying to tell you. Negotiations can be tricky. I was prohibited from saying anything until we'd reached an agreement with Dalton Publishing and the financing had been arranged."

Steffie snuggled down against her pillows. "So much is happening in our lives. First there was Dad's heart attack, and now Valerie's wedding. Oh, Charles, I wish you were here to see Valerie. I didn't know anything in the world could fluster my sister, but I was wrong. Being in love flusters her.

"I was with her Monday when she tried on wedding dresses. My practical, levelheaded older sister would stand in front of a mirror with huge tears running down her cheeks."

"She was crying?"

Steffie smiled at the memory. "Yes, but these were tears of joy. She never allowed herself to believe that Colby loved her enough to work through the things that stood between them. They're so different, and that's been the problem all along. But neither of them seems to understand, even now, that it was those very differences that attracted them to each other.''

''We're different.''

His words gave Steffie pause. ''I know but—''

''And I'm attracted to you, Stephanie. Very attracted.''

It was ironic that she'd told him how love had completely unsettled her sister, only to be sitting on her own bed a few minutes later with the phone pressed against her ear and the tears sliding down her cheeks.

''Aren't you going to say anything?''

''Yes,'' she whispered in a trembling voice.

''Stephanie? What's wrong? You sound like you're crying.''

''That's the silliest thing I ever heard,'' she rallied, rubbing her eyes with one hand.

''Damn, but I wish I was there.''

''Sorry,'' she said laughing and crying at once, ''you're flat out of wishes.''

CHAPTER EIGHT

"MORE WINE?" Charles asked, reaching for the bottle of Chablis in its silver bucket.

"No, thanks," Steffie said, smiling her appreciation. Their dinner had been delectable. It was one meal she wouldn't soon forget, although it was Charles's company that would linger in her mind more than the excellent halibut topped with bay shrimp.

"How about dessert?"

Steffie pressed her hands to her stomach and slowly shook her head. "I couldn't."

"Me neither." He leaned against the back of his chair and gazed out the window to the Columbia River below. The gorge stretched through one of the most scenic parts of Oregon. Steffie had always loved this view of the mighty river coursing through a rockbound corridor.

"I've looked forward to this evening for a long time," Charles said, looking back at her.

"I have, too." Until tonight, Steffie had only dreamed of spending time like this with Charles. As his equal, an adult . . . a woman in love.

"I don't think I've ever seen you look more beautiful, Stephanie."

His words brought a flush of color to her cheeks. Steffie had dressed carefully, choosing a soft Italian knit dress in a subdued shade of turquoise. Small rhinestones drizzled over the shoulders and spilled down the front. Valerie had lent Steffie her pearl necklace and earrings, and Norah had contributed a splash of her most expensive perfume.

It seemed her sisters and her father, too, had put a good deal of stock into this evening's dinner date. Steffie wasn't entirely sure what her family was expecting would happen. No doubt some miracle. For herself, she was content just to spend the evening with Charles

"You look wonderful yourself." She wasn't echoing his compliment, but was stating a fact. He'd worn a dark, double-breasted suit with a silk tie of swirling colors against a pale blue shirt.

"Then we must make an attractive couple tonight," Charles commented, rotating the wine goblet between his fingers.

"We must," Steffie agreed.

Charles finished off the last of his wine and set the glass aside. "You were generous enough to grant me three wishes the other night, remember?"

Steffie wasn't likely to forget. She felt warm and shivery inside whenever she thought about their late-night telephone conversation.

"Being the honorable gentleman I am, not to mention talented and handsome, as you so aptly pointed out, it seems only fair that I return the favor. You, my lady, are hereby granted three wishes."

"Anything I want?" Steffie cocked her head.

"Within reason. I'd be willing to drive you to Multnomah Falls to watch the water by moonlight, but I might have a bit of trouble if you decide you want world peace."

"The Falls by moonlight?"

"I was hoping you'd ask for that one."

She blinked at the way he'd turned her question into a pre-approved wish. "Charles," she said surprised, "you're a romantic."

"Don't sound so shocked."

"But I am. I'd never have guessed it."

She was teasing him, and enjoying it and was surprised when he frowned briefly. "That's because we've never discussed what happened three—"

"Not tonight," she said, holding a finger to his lips. "It's one of my wishes. We'll discuss nothing unpleasant."

His frown deepened. "I think we should. There's a lot we—"

"You're the one who granted me three wishes," she reminded him solemnly.

He nodded, looking somewhat disgruntled. "You're right, I did, and if you want to squander one of your wishes, then far be it from me to stop you."

"It's too lovely a night to dredge up the past, especially when it's so embarrassing. Let's just look forward..."

"Fine," Charles agreed and turned to thank their waiter when he brought two cups of steaming coffee to the table. "We'll just look ahead. Now, remember you have one remaining wish."

Steffie hesitated. "Do I have to claim it now?"

"No, but the wishes expire at midnight."

Steffie laughed softly. "You make me feel like Cinderella."

"Perhaps that's because I'd like to be your prince."

His gaze was dark and unguarded. Steffie lowered her eyes, for fear he would read all the love that was stored in her heart.

"Do I frighten you?" he asked after a moment.

Steffie's gaze flew back to his. "No. I thought I frightened you!"

He laughed outright at that. "Not likely."

They drank their coffee in silence, as though afraid words would destroy the mood. After Charles had paid the bill, he drove toward Multnomah Falls, managing the twisting narrow highway with ease. Steffie had visited Multnomah Falls many times, but had always been a bit frightened by the drive. However, Charles took the sharp turns in slow, easy moves, and she relaxed, enjoying the trip.

The rock walls along the road were built of local basalt more than fifty years earlier, during the Depression.

"I love this place," Charles said as they reached the parking area across the roadway from the waterfall. Because it was a week night, there were only a few cars parked in the lot.

Dusk was settling, and the tall, stately firs bordering the falls were silhouetted against the backdrop of a cloud-dappled sky. The forested slopes were already dark as Steffie and Charles began the gradual, winding ascent to the visitors' viewpoint.

A chill raced down her arms and Steffie was grateful she'd brought a thin coat with her. Multnomah Falls was Oregon's highest waterfall, plummeting more than six hundred feet into a swirling pool, then slipping downward in a second, shorter descent. The force of the falling water misted the night.

With his hand at her elbow, Charles guided them to the walkway that wove its way up the trail. When they reached the footbridge that spanned the falls, Steffie stopped to gaze at the magnificence around her. The sound of falling water roared in her ears.

"If we wait a few moments, the moon will hit the water," Charles told her. He stood behind her, shielding her from the wind that whipped across the water's churning surface.

Steffie closed her eyes. Not to the beauty of the scene before her, but to the sensation she experienced in Charles's protective embrace.

"I've dreamed of holding you like this," he whispered. "Of wrapping my arms around you and feeling you next to me. I love the way your hair smells. It reminds me of wildflowers and sunshine."

Steffie couldn't speak. She couldn't force even one word past the knot in her throat. She swallowed and slowed her breathing, hoping that might help, for there was so much she longed to say, so many things she yearned to tell him.

"I don't ever want to be separated from you again,"
Charles told her, his voice raw and painful.

She didn't understand. Charles had all but sent her
away. He'd all but cast her out of his life. She turned
in his arms until they faced each other and raised her
hands to his face.

Charles smiled then and gently gripped her wrists.
He moved his head until his mouth met the sensitive
skin of her palm, and he kissed her there.

"You know, three years ago there was so much I
couldn't tell you," he began.

"I have one wish left," she reminded him softly. "I
want you to kiss me. Now."

"With pleasure." She could hear the smile in his
voice.

They'd kissed before, but they'd never shared what
they did in those few moments. Charles's lips found
hers in the sweetest, most loving exchange she'd ever
experienced, and Steffie's emotions exploded to life.

Steffie wanted this, wanted it more than anything
she'd ever known, yet at the same time she felt
swamped by confusion. Charles had ordered her out
of his life, laughed at her declaration of love, humiliated her until she couldn't bear to live in the same
town. Now, he seemed to be suggesting that he *hadn't*
wanted her to go, and that he never wanted her to leave
again.

Steffie wasn't sure what to believe. With all her
heart she longed to lose herself in Charles's kiss, to
savor all the sensations that flooded her. And yet the

uncertainty remained. Did he merely desire her, or did he, too, feel a forever kind of love?

But his kiss wiped out all thought, as the joy rushed through her, replacing fear and doubt.

"Someone's coming," Charles whispered suddenly. He broke away, still holding her shoulders, and gently brushed his mouth against her forehead. Then he released her.

STEFFIE'S FATHER was sitting by the fireplace in his den when she let herself into the house later that night. She saw the lamplight spilling into the entryway and decided to check on him.

"Dad?" David was sitting in the wingback leather chair beside the fireplace, her mother's afghan tucked around his legs. His head drooped and his lips were slightly parted.

Steffie had spoken before she realized he was asleep. But just as she turned to tiptoe from the room, he stirred.

"Steffie?"

"I didn't mean to wake you," she told him softly.

"Good thing you did. I was waiting for you." He ran one hand through his hair and sat up straighter. "How was your dinner with Charles?"

Steffie sank onto the ottoman, angling her legs to one side. She knew her eyes had a dreamy look, but she didn't care. "Wonderful."

"Did Charles ask you anything?"

"Ask me anything?" she repeated, feigning ignorance. "What could he possibly have to ask me?"

David Bloomfield frowned. "Plenty. I thought—I hoped he was going to mention a wedding. Yours."

"Oh, that!" she said with a light disinterested laugh. If the evening hadn't been so wonderful, she would have felt irritated with his pressure tactics. But she found it impossible to complain when she was this happy.

"He did, you mean? And what did you tell him? Don't keep me in suspense, Princess."

Steffie splayed her fingers and studied the even, smoothly polished nails before sighing. "I told him we'll see about it on Sunday."

"Sunday? You're going to keep that dear boy in agony until Sunday?"

She nodded, affecting a complete lack of concern. "He wanted to know if we could go horseback riding, and I said we could probably do it on Sunday. That's the question you're referring to, isn't it?"

"No," came his disappointed reply. "And well you know it. I expected that boy to ask you to marry him."

"Well, he didn't and even if he had—"

"Even if he had, what?" The frown slid back into place. "I tell you, Stephanie, you're as stubborn as your mother when it comes to this sort of thing. You can't fool me—you've been in love with Charles for years. If he asked you to marry him—"

"But he hasn't and from what I could see, he doesn't have any intention of doing so."

"I don't agree."

"You're free to think what you want, Dad, but keep in mind that this is *my* life and I won't take kindly to your interfering in it. And remember that Charles values his privacy, too.''

"He didn't ask you to marry him," her father muttered under his breath. "You don't think he intends to, either?" he demanded, louder now.

"Not to the best of my knowledge."

A look of righteous indignation came over her father's face. "Then I'd best have a talk with that boy. I won't allow him to trifle with your affections."

"Dad!" Steffie had trouble not laughing over the old-fashioned terms he used. She was sure Charles would find it humorous, too, if she suggested he was trifling with her heart.

"I mean it, Steffie. I refuse to allow that young man to hurt you again."

"He only has that power if I give it to him—which I won't. You're looking at a woman of the nineties, Dad, and we're too smart to let a man *trifle* with us."

"Nevertheless, I'd better have a talk with him."

Her expression might have been outwardly serene, but Steffie's insides were dancing a wild jig. "You'll do no such thing," she insisted.

"Apparently Charles Tomaselli doesn't know what's good for him."

"Dad! We talked about this before, remember?" Her good mood was quickly evaporating. "Now I want you to promise you're not going to interfere with Charles and me."

Her father stubbornly refused to answer.

"I'd be mortified if you even bring up the subject of marriage to him."

"But—"

"I'm trusting you, Dad. Now good night." She stood and kissed his brow before heading up the stairs to her own bedroom.

"I APPRECIATE the ride to the airport," Valerie said as they drove out of town early Saturday afternoon. Her sister's flight was scheduled to leave at five, which gave them plenty of time for a leisurely trip into Portland. Valerie was going to meet with Rowdy Cassidy to tell him about her engagement and request a job transfer.

"I'm glad to do it," Steffie assured her older sister. Now that Valerie had set the preparations for her wedding in motion, she was free to return to Texas. There were several tasks, besides the discussion with Cassidy, that she needed to take care of. She had to pack her personal things, deal with her furniture and put her condo on the market.

"Colby wanted to come with me, but his schedule's full," she explained wistfully. "That's something we're both going to have to adjust to."

"Heavy schedules?"

Valerie nodded. "I'll need to talk to Rowdy about that while I'm in Houston."

"Do you think he'll agree to let you head up the West Coast branch of CHIPS?"

"It's hard to say.... I don't think he's going to be pleased about my wanting to leave Houston, but he hasn't got a choice." Steffie noticed a hesitancy in her sister that she hadn't seen earlier. "Rowdy can be hard to predict," Valerie added. "He might be absolutely delighted for me and Colby. But there's also a chance that he'll be angry I took an extended leave of absence to plan my wedding.'' She sighed. ''I didn't tell him the whole truth about why I didn't return the day I said I would.''

''Why not?'' Steffie prodded, briefly taking her eyes from the road when Valerie didn't immediately offer the information.

''I know I should have, but it just didn't seem the thing to do over the phone. Besides, I'm afraid Rowdy might be...have been interested in me himself. At one point, I even thought I was interested in him! Good heavens, I didn't know a thing about love until I met Colby. I don't mean to hurt Rowdy's feelings but I can't give him any hope.''

''Do you want me to fly back with you?''

''Oh, no. Rowdy's really a gentleman beneath that rough-and-tough cowboy exterior.''

Steffie's suspicions were raised. ''Does the good doctor know how Rowdy feels about you?''

''I think he might. Then again we've never really discussed Rowdy, and why should we? If you want the truth, I think Colby would rather forget about him.''

''Maybe he should take his head out of the sand.''

''Now don't you go saying anything to him,'' Valerie said vehemently. ''I mean it, Steff. What happens between Rowdy and me is between Rowdy and me.''

''Is Colby the jealous type?'' Steffie remembered how she'd felt the day she found Charles standing next to Wendy, the apprentice at the *Clarion*. Until that moment, she'd never thought of herself as jealous. Even now the blood simmered in her veins when she recalled how the little blonde had gazed up at Charles, her blue eyes wide with open admiration.

"I don't know if Colby is or not. I only know how I'd feel if the situation was reversed." Valerie seemed to consider her next words. "Before Colby and I became engaged he was dating a nurse. I believe she's a friend of Norah's. Apparently he'd been going out with her for quite a while. Everyone was expecting them to announce their engagement. Norah seemed to feel otherwise, but that's another story."

"I swear Norah's got a sixth sense about these things."

Valerie nodded. "I think she does, too. At any rate, Colby and I decided that although we were attracted to each other, a long-term relationship was out of the question. Colby...asked me to hurry up and leave because my staying made everything so much more painful for us both."

"He didn't!" Steffie was outraged. "It's a good thing he didn't say that around me."

Valerie laughed. "He didn't really mean it. Oh, maybe he did at the time, but I didn't make falling in love easy for either of us."

Valerie's stubbornness was a trait the three Bloomfield sisters shared, Steffie thought with a small, rueful grin.

"After we talked, Colby started dating Sherry again. I think they went out four or five nights in a row. I didn't know about it, but in a way, I guess I did. I certainly wasn't surprised when I heard.

"Poor Norah felt she had to let me know what was happening. I think it was harder on her than on me."

"Were you jealous?"

"That's the funny part," Valerie said pensively. "At first I was so jealous I wanted to scratch out Sherry's eyes. I fantasized about hunting down Colby Winston and making him suffer."

"You should have asked me to help you. I'd have gladly volunteered."

Valerie smiled and patted Steffie's forearm. "Spoken like a true sister, but as I said that was my *first* reaction. What I found interesting was that it didn't last.

"I sat down and thought about it and realized how selfish and unfair I was being to Colby. If I truly loved him, I should want him to have whatever made him happy. If that meant marriage to Sherry Waterman, then so be it."

"In other words you were willing to let him go."

"Yes. And that was a turning point for me. Don't misunderstand me, it hurt more than anything I've ever done. Remember the day I was scheduled to fly back to Houston?"

Steffie wasn't likely to forget it. "Of course."

"When I first got ready to leave, I really had to work at controlling myself. I wasn't sure I could make it down the front steps without bursting into tears."

"I knew you were upset . . ."

"Naturally, Colby would have to choose right then to stop in for a visit. That man's sense of timing is going to be a big problem.'' Valerie shook her head in mock exasperation.

Steffie laughed. Give Valerie a week and she'd have Colby's life completely reorganized.

''Somehow I managed to pull it off,'' Valerie continued. ''I remember sitting in the car and—this is odd—I felt such a sense of peace. I don't know if I can explain it. I felt this incredible . . . nobility. Don't you dare laugh, Steffie, I'm serious. I didn't stop loving Colby—if anything, I found I loved him more. Here I was, willingly walking away from the first man I'd ever loved.''

''I wanted to throttle Colby about then.''

Valerie grinned. ''I remember learning about the tragic hero in my college literature courses. In some ways, I felt like I qualified for the tragic heroine.''

''You weren't sorry you'd fallen in love with him, were you?''

''No, I was grateful. I was leaving him and at the same time I was giving him permission to find his own joy. And like I said, that somehow . . . ennobled me.''

Steffie recalled the farewell scene on her front porch when she'd been so angry with Colby. ''I . . . don't know if I could be so noble when it came to Charles.''

''What's happening with the two of you?''

''I don't know.'' Steffie was being entirely honest. ''We had a wonderful evening on Thursday, then we drove to Multnomah Falls and watched the moonlight on the water.''

''That sounds so romantic.''

"It was. We walked up to the footbridge and... talked."

"I'll bet!" Valerie laughed.

"We did—only we did more kissing than talking." Steffie knew that Charles had wanted to talk, wanted to discuss the past with her. She hated the thought of reliving all that pain. But more than anything she dreaded examining her utterly ridiculous behavior. Every time she recalled the scene in his bathroom, with her playing the role of enchantress, she burned with humiliation. Someday they'd talk about it, but not now. It was too soon.

"Dad seems to think you two will get married."

This discussion was a repeat of the one she'd had with her father every day for the past two weeks. "You know Dad when he's got a bee in his bonnet. I've had to make him promise he wouldn't say a word about marriage to Charles."

"Do you honestly believe he listened to you?" Valerie wanted to know.

"He'd better have."

Valerie frowned as she turned to stare out the car window. Steffie's hands closed tightly on the steering wheel and she glanced around her. Wild rhododendrons blossomed along the side of the roadway, their bright pink flowers a colorful contrast to the lush green foliage.

"I'm worried about Dad."

Valerie's words surprised Steffie. "Why? He's getting stronger every day. His recovery is nothing short of miraculous. I've heard you say so yourself, at least a dozen times."

"All right, I'll rephrase that. I'm worried for you."

"Me? Whatever for?" As far as Steffie was concerned, her life had rarely been better. She'd applied for late admission to the Ph.D. program and planned to begin researching thesis topics soon; she'd temporarily put her career plans on hold. And as for Charles . . . well, things were wonderful. Yes, she still had a lot of murky ground to cover with him, but there'd be time for that later.

"Dad's riding high on success," Valerie reminded her. "He seems to think that because everything fell into place with Colby and me, it should for you and Charles, as well. Remember he's supposed to have dreamed all this."

"I know. We've had our go-arounds on that issue. He's told me at least twice a day for the past two weeks that I'm going to marry Charles by the end of the summer. It's gotten to where I just smile and nod and let him think what he wants."

"It doesn't bother you?"

"It drives me nuts." Possibly because she wanted to believe it so badly.

"Aren't you nervous that Dad's going to get impatient and say something to Charles?"

"No," Steffie answered automatically. "Dad and I've been over this. He knows better than to say anything to Charles."

Valerie nodded. "I wish I shared your confidence."

Steffie put on a good front for the remainder of the trip, but she was growing more and more concerned. She knew one thing; she didn't have the personality to play the role of tragic heroine. She'd leave that to her older, wiser sister.

The flight was on time, and as soon as Valerie boarded the plane for Texas, Steffie headed back to Orchard Valley. As the minutes ticked away, she became increasingly anxious to get home.

It was just like Valerie to plant the seeds of doubt and then fly off, leaving Steffie to deal with the result—a garden full of weeds!

When she pulled into the driveway, Steffie experienced an immediate sense of relief. Her world was in order; her fears shrank to nothing. All was well. Her father was rocking on the front porch, the way he did every evening. He smiled and waved when he saw her.

"Hello, good lookin'," she said as she climbed out of the car. "How was your day?"

"I had a great afternoon. Every day's wonderful now that I've got all these reasons to live. Oh, before I forget, Charles stopped by to see you. Guess he must've been in the neighborhood again." A smile twinkled from her father's eyes. "You might give him a call. I suspect he's waiting to hear from you."

Steffie froze. Doubt sprang to new life. "You didn't say anything to him about . . . what we discussed, did you?"

"Princess, I didn't say a word you wouldn't want me to."

"You're sure?"

"As positive as I'm sitting here."

Steffie went inside the house, reassured by her father's words. Norah was busy in the kitchen, kneading bread dough on a lightly floured countertop.

"Did you happen to see Charles?" Steffie asked in passing. She opened the refrigerator and removed a cold soda.

"He stopped by earlier and sat on the porch with Dad for a while. I don't think he was here more than fifteen minutes."

Steffie swallowed a long cool drink. "I'll give him a call."

"Sounds like a good idea."

She waited until she was in her room, then sat on her bed and reached for the phone. Although it had been several years since she'd called Charles, she still remembered his number. The same way she remembered everything else about him.

He must have been sitting by the phone, because he answered even before the first ring was finished.

"Charles, hello," she said happily. "Dad said you stopped by."

"Yes, I did."

His voice was cool, and Steffie paused as the dread took hold inside her. "Is something wrong?"

"Not wrong, exactly. I guess you could say I'm disappointed. I thought you'd changed, Steffie. I thought you'd grown up and stopped your naive tricks. But I was wrong, wasn't I?"

CHAPTER NINE

"DAD!" Steffie struggled to keep the anger and distress out of her voice. She hurried to the front porch, her fists clenched against her sides. "You told me... you promised..." She hesitated. "What *exactly* did you say to Charles?"

Her father glanced upward momentarily, clearly puzzled. "Nothing drastic, I assure you. Is it important?"

"Yes, it's important! I need to know." It required every ounce of self-control she possessed not to shout at him and demand an explanation. She longed to chastise him for doing the very thing she'd begged him not to.

"You look upset, Princess."

"I am upset and I'm sure you know why... Just tell me what you said to Charles."

"Sit down a bit and we'll talk."

Steffie did as her father requested, sitting on the top porch step near his chair and leaning back against the white pillar. "Charles stopped in this afternoon, right?"

"Yes, and we had a nice chat. He tried to let me think he was here to visit me, but I saw through that soon enough." Her father's smile told Steffie all she needed to know. For one angry second, she thought he resembled a spider, patiently waiting for someone to step into his web.

"Obviously I was the subject under discussion, right?" She forced herself not to yell, not to rant and rave at a man so recently released from the hospital.

Her father rocked back and forth a few times, then nodded. "We talked about you."

Steffie closed her eyes, her frustration mounting. "I see. And what did the two of you come up with?"

"Let me tell you what Charles said first."

She balled her hands into fists again, praying for patience. *"What did he say?"*

"Well, Charles stopped by, as I said, pretending it was me he was here to visit, when we both knew he was coming to see you. I went along with him for a while, then asked him flat-out what his intentions were toward you. I fully expected you to be wearing an engagement ring by now, and I let him know it."

"Dad!" Without meaning to, Steffie sprang to her feet. "You breached a trust! I trusted you to keep your word, not to talk to Charles about this. And now you pass it off as...as nothing. Don't you realize what you've done?"

For the first time he looked chagrined. "I did it because I love you, Princess."

"Oh, Dad...you've made everything so much more difficult."

"Aren't you interested in what he had to say?" His smile was bright and cocky again. "Well, aren't you? Now sit back down and I'll tell you."

"Oh, all right," she muttered, lowering herself onto the porch step, her legs barely able to support her. Already she was shaking with trepidation.

"Charles seemed more concerned with the fact that I'd asked than with answering the question. To be perfectly honest, Princess, he wasn't overly pleased with me."

"I can't believe he even answered you."

"Of course he did. He said if the subject of marriage did come up, then it was between the two of you, and not the three of us. It was a good response."

"You should never have said anything about us marrying."

"Well, Princess, the way I figured it, he was going to pop the question, anyway. Besides, I don't want Charles leading you on, or hurting you again."

"Dad, you've made it nearly impossible for me and—"

"Let me finish, because there's more to tell you." But after silencing her, he went strangely quiet himself.

"Go on," she urged, clenching her jaw.

"I'm just trying to think of a way to tell you this without annoying you even more. I told Charles something you didn't want me to tell him."

"The dream?" The question came out a whisper. "But you said you hadn't told Charles anything I

wouldn't want you to. And before—you *promised* you
wouldn't mention marriage!''

"No, Princess, I never did promise. I took it under
consideration, but not once did I actually say I
wouldn't discuss this with Charles. Now don't look so
worried. I didn't tell him a thing about talking to your
mother, or about the three precious children the two
of you will be having someday.''

"What did Charles say? No,'' she amended quickly,
"tell me *exactly* what you said first.''

"Well, as I said, we were chatting—''

"Get to the part where you mentioned marriage.''

"All right, all right. But I want you to know I didn't
tell him about the dream. Not because you didn't want
me to, but because when it came right down to it, I
didn't think he'd believe me. You three girls are having trouble enough, so I can hardly expect someone
outside the family to listen.''

"You told Colby about it.''

"Of course I did. He's my doctor. He had a right to
know.''

"Great. In other words you blurted out that you
expected Charles to marry me—because you didn't
want him trifling with my heart?'' Spoken aloud, it
sounded so ludicrous. Not to mention insulting. No
wonder Charles was cool toward her.

"Not exactly. I asked his intentions. He said that
was between the two of you. As I already told you.''

"Good.'' Steffie relaxed somewhat. "And that was
the end of it?'' she murmured hopefully.

"Not entirely.''

"What else is there?"

"I told him you were anticipating a proposal of marriage, and for that matter so was I."

Steffie ground her teeth to keep from screaming out her irritation. It was worse than she'd feared. Sagging against the pillar, she covered her face with both hands. It would have been far better had he told Charles about the dream. That way, Charles might have understood that she'd had nothing to do with this. Instead, her father had made everything ten times worse by *not* mentioning it.

Charles was angry with her; that was obvious from their telephone conversation. He'd refused to discuss it in any detail, just repeating that he was "disappointed." He seemed to believe she'd manipulated her father into approaching him with this marriage business. He wasn't likely to change his mind unless she could convince him of the truth.

"Where are you going?" her father asked when she left him and returned a moment later with her purse and a sweater.

"To talk to Charles—to explain things, if I can."

"Good." David's grin was full. "All that boy needs is a bit of prompting. You wait and see. Once you get back, you'll thank me for taking matters into my own hands. There's something about making a commitment to the right woman that fixes everything."

Steffie was drained from the emotion. She found she couldn't remain angry with her father. He'd talked to Charles with the best motives, the best intentions. And he didn't know what had gone on between her and

Charles in the past—the tricks she'd played. So he couldn't possibly understand why Charles would react with such anger to being pressed on the issue of marriage.

"I'll wait up for you and when you get home we'll celebrate together," he suggested.

Steffie grinned weakly and nodded, but she doubted there'd be anything to celebrate.

SHE TOOK HER TIME driving into town, using those minutes to organize her thoughts. She hoped Charles would be open-minded enough to accept her explanation. Mostly, she wanted to reassure him that she hadn't talked her father into interrogating him about marriage. They'd come so far in the past few weeks, she and Charles, and Steffie didn't want anything to spoil that.

Charles was waiting for her, or he seemed to be. She'd barely rung his doorbell when he answered.

"Hello." His immediate appearance took her by surprise. "I—I thought it might be a good idea if the two of us sat down and talked."

"Fine." He didn't smile, didn't show any sign of pleasure at seeing her.

"Dad told me he talked to you about . . . the two of us marrying." The words felt awkward on her tongue.

"He did mention something along those lines," Charles returned stiffly.

He hadn't asked her to make herself comfortable or motioned her to sit down. It didn't matter, though, since she couldn't stand still, anyway. She paced from one side of his living room to the other. She felt strangely chilled, despite the warm spring weather.

"You think I put Dad up to it, don't you?"

"Yes," he said frankly.

He stood rooted to the same spot while she drifted, apparently aimlessly, around the room. His look, everything about him, wasn't encouraging. Perhaps she should have delayed this, let them both sleep on it, instead of forcing the issue. Perhaps she should have dropped the entire thing, and let this misunderstanding sort itself out. Perhaps she should go home now before everything got much worse.

"I didn't ask Dad to say anything to you," she told him simply.

"I wish I could believe that."

"Why can't you? This is ridiculous. If you intend to drag the past into every disagreement, punish me for something that happened three years ago, then—"

"I'm not talking about three years ago. I'm talking about here and now."

"What do you mean?"

"I'll say this for you, Steffie, you've gotten far more subtle."

"How...do you mean?"

"First, you park in front of the newspaper office just as I happen to be—"

"When?"

"Last week. I was talking to Wendy, and when I looked up, I saw you sitting in your car, staring at us. Just how long had you been there?"

"I...don't know."

"Now that I think about it, I realize what a fool I've been. You've been spying on me for weeks, haven't you?"

The idea was so outlandish that Steffie found herself laughing incredulously. Nothing she said would matter anymore, not if he believed what he was saying now. Because if he did, there was nothing of their relationship left to salvage.

"There's no fooling you, is there?" she threw out sarcastically. "You're much too smart for me, Charles. I've been hiding around town for days, following you with binoculars, charting your activities. It's amazing you didn't catch on sooner."

He ignored her scornful remarks. "It was convenient the way you twisted your ankle the other day, too, wasn't it? Somehow you managed to fall directly into my arms."

"The timing was perfect, wasn't it?" she said with a short, humorless laugh. "You're right, I couldn't have planned that any better."

He frowned. "Then there was the dinner waiting for me at the house the other night. Italian, too, just the way my grandmother used to make it."

"Amazing how I knew that, isn't it?"

"All this adds up to one thing."

"And what might that be?" she asked scathingly, folding her arms and cocking her head. She'd assumed far too much in this relationship. She'd lowered her guard and actually believed Charles loved her, because she loved him so deeply. Now she realized how wrong she'd been.

"It adds up to the fact that you're playing games again."

"Don't forget the moonlight the night we were at Multnomah Falls. I arranged that, too, along with everything else. I have to admit it took some doing, but I'm a clever soul."

"There's no need to be sarcastic."

"I don't agree," she returned defiantly.

Charles frowned and muttered something she couldn't understand.

"I must say I'm surprised you caught on so quickly, what with me being so subtle and all."

"Let's clear the air once and—"

"But the air *is* clear," she said, waving her arms wildly. She knew she was going too far with this, but the momentum was building and she couldn't seem to stop. "I've been found out, and now it's all over."

"Over?"

"Of course. There's no need to pretend any longer."

"What are you talking about?"

"Revenge. It's supposed to be sweet, and it would have been if you hadn't caught on when you did."

"Just what did you intend to do?" he demanded.

"You mean you don't have that figured out, as well?"

"Tell me, Stephanie." His voice was hard as ice and just as cold.

"All right, if you must know. Once I got you to the point of proposing—" she paused dramatically "—I was going to laugh and reject you. It seems only fair after the way you humiliated me. You laughed at me,

Charles, and it was going to be my turn to laugh at you. Only you found me out first...."

His frown deepened into a scowl. "Your father—"

"Oh, don't worry, he didn't know anything about that part. Getting him to shame you into a marriage proposal was tricky, but I managed it by telling him I was afraid you were trifling with my affections." She gave a deep exaggerated sigh, astonished that he seemed to believe all this.

"I see."

"Oh, you're too clever for me, Charles. What can I possibly say? There's no need to pretend any more."

"Perhaps it would be best if you left now."

"I think you're right. Well, at least you know what it feels like to have someone laugh at you."

Charles walked to his front door and held it open for her. With a jaunty step, Steffie walked out of his house. "Well, I'll see you around, but you don't need to worry—I won't be spying on you anymore."

His jaw was tightly clamped, and Steffie realized she'd succeeded beyond all her expectations. Charles was disgusted with her. And furious. So furious that he couldn't get her out of his home fast enough.

"You can't blame a girl for trying," she said with a shrug once she'd slipped past him.

In response, Charles slammed his door shut.

By the time Steffie was inside the car, she was shaking so badly that she could barely insert the key into the ignition. Her breath seemed to be caught in her chest, creating a painful need to exhale.

Like Charles, she was angry, more angry than she'd ever been in her life. In one rational corner of her mind, she knew—had known all along—that it was a mistake to goad him with all those ridiculous lies.

But the amazing thing, the sad thing, was that he'd believed them. To his way of thinking, apparently, it all fit. And as far as Steffie was concerned, there was nothing more to say.

In time, she'd regret her outburst, but she didn't then. At that moment, she was far too infuriated to care. In time, she'd regret the lies, the squandered hopes—but it wouldn't be anytime soon.

"WELL?" her father asked, his expression pleased and expectant as she let herself into the house an hour later. "Are you two going to look for an engagement ring in the next few days?"

"Not exactly," Steffie said, moving into his den. As he'd promised earlier, her father was waiting up for her, reading in his favorite chair.

His face fell with disappointment. "But you did talk about getting married, didn't you?"

"Not really. We, uh, got sidetracked."

"You didn't argue, did you?"

"Not really." Steffie was unsure how much to tell her father. She worried that if he realized the extent of the rift between her and Charles, he'd feel obliged to do something to patch things up.

David set aside his reading glasses and gazed up at her. "You'll be seeing him again soon, won't you?"

Living in Orchard Valley made that highly likely. It was the very reason she'd chosen to study in Europe three years earlier. "Naturally I'll be seeing him."

David nodded, appeased. "Good."

"I think I'll go up to my room and read. Good night, Dad."

"Night, Princess."

As it happened, Steffie met Norah at the top of the stairs. Her younger sister glanced her way and did an automatic double-take. "What's wrong?"

"What makes you think something's wrong?"

"You mean other than the fact that you look like you're waiting to get to your room before you cry?"

Her sister knew her too well. Steffie felt terrible—discouraged, disheartened, depressed. But in her present mood, she didn't have the patience to explain what had happened between her and Charles.

"What could possibly be wrong?" Steffie asked instead, feigning a lightness she didn't feel.

"Funny you should say that," Norah said, tucking her arm through Steffie's and leading the way to her bedroom. "Valerie asked me nearly the same thing not so long ago. What could possibly be wrong? Well, I'd have to say it was probably trouble with a man."

"That's very astute of you."

"Obviously it's Charles, then." Norah didn't react to Steffie's mild sarcasm.

"Obviously." She was tired, weary all the way to her bones and desperately craving a long, hot soak in the tub. Some of her best thinking was accomplished while lazing in a bathtub filled with scented water. She'd avoided bubble baths since the time she'd spent hours in one waiting for Charles.

"Did you two have a spat?"

"Not exactly. Listen, Norah, I appreciate your concern—really, I do... I don't mean to sound ungrateful, but I'm tired and I want to go to bed."

"Bed? Good grief, it's barely seven."

"It's been a long day."

Norah eyed her suspiciously. "It must have been."

"Besides I have a busy day scheduled for Monday."

Norah's interest was piqued. "What's happening then?"

"I'm going to Portland to see about my application at the university and to find an apartment."

For a moment Norah said nothing. Her mouth fell open and she wore a stunned look. "But I thought you told Dad you were going to wait on that."

"I was..."

"But you aren't any longer? Even after you promised Dad?"

Steffie glanced away, not wanting her sister to realize how deeply hurt she was. How betrayed she felt that Charles would believe she was so deceitful as to trick him into marriage. It seemed that whenever Charles Tomaselli was involved, she invariably ended up in pain.

"I FEEL BETTER than I have in years." David greeted Steffie cheerfully early the next morning. He was sitting at the kitchen table, drinking a cup of coffee and going over the Portland edition of the Sunday paper. He welcomed her with a warm smile, apparently not noticing his daughter's lackluster mood. "It's a beautiful morning," David added.

"Beautiful," Steffie mumbled as she poured herself a cup of coffee and staggered to the table. Her eyes burned from lack of sleep, and she felt as though she were walking around in a nightmare.

She'd spent the entire night arguing with herself about the lies she'd told Charles. In the end, she'd managed to convince herself that she'd done the right thing. Charles *wanted* to believe every word. He'd seized every one of her sarcastic remarks, all too ready to consider them truth.

"What time will Charles be by?" her father asked conversationally.

"Charles?" She repeated his name as though she'd never heard it before.

"I thought the two of you were going horseback riding sometime this afternoon."

"Uh...I'm not sure Charles will be able to come, after all." The date had probably slipped his mind, the way it had hers. Even if he did remember, Steffie sincerely doubted he'd show up. As far as she was concerned, whatever had been between them was over now. In fact, the more she reviewed their last discussion, the angrier she became. If he honestly believed the things she'd suggested—and he certainly seemed to—then there was no hope for them. None.

"I'd better get dressed for church," Steffie said bleakly.

"You've got plenty of time yet."

"Norah has to get there early." Her sister sang in the choir. Generally Norah left the house before the others, but Steffie thought she'd ride with Norah this morning, if for no better reason than to escape her father's questions. From the looks David was giving her, he was sure to subject her to a full-scale inquisition if she stayed in the kitchen much longer.

Attending church was an uplifting experience for Steffie. During that hour, she was able to forget her troubles and absorb the atmosphere of peace and serenity. Whatever solace she found, however, vanished the minute she and Norah drove into the yard shortly after noon.

Charles's car was parked out front.

Steffie tensed and released a long, slow sigh.

"Problems?" Norah asked.

"I don't know."

"Do you want to talk to him?"

It didn't take Steffie more than a moment to decide. "No, I don't." But at the same time, she wasn't about to back down, either. She wouldn't allow Charles to chase her from her own home. He was on her turf now, and she didn't run easily.

Steffie parked behind Charles's sports car and willed herself to remain calm and collected. Her father must have heard them because he stepped outside the house, his welcoming smile in place. He still moved slowly but with increasing confidence. It was sometimes hard to remember that he was recovering from major surgery.

"Steffie, Charles is here."

"So I see," she said with a decided lack of enthusiasm.

"He's in the stable, waiting for you."

She nodded and, with her heart racing wildly, walked up the steps and past her father.

"Aren't you going to talk to him?"

"I need to change my clothes first."

"To talk? But..." He hesitated, then reluctantly nodded.

By the time Steffie was in her bedroom, she was trembling. Her emotions were so confused that she wasn't sure if she was shaking with anger or with nervousness. But she did know she wasn't ready to face him, wasn't ready to deal with his accusations or his reproach. For several minutes she sat on her bed, trying to decide what to do.

"Steffie." Norah stood in the doorway, watching her, looking concerned. "Are you all right?"

"Of course I—no, I'm not," she said. "I'm not ready to talk to Charles yet."

"Nothing says you have to talk to him if you don't want to. I'll make up some excuse and send him packing."

"No." For pride's sake, she didn't want him to know how badly she'd been hurt by their latest confrontation.

"You look like you're about to dissolve into tears."

Steffie squared her shoulders and met her sister's worried gaze. "I'm not going to give him the satisfaction."

"Atta girl," Norah said approvingly.

Changing into jeans and a sweatshirt, Steffie went down the back stairs into the kitchen. She didn't expect to find Charles sitting at the table chatting with her father. The sight took her by surprise. What unsettled her most was that he gave no outward sign of their quarrel. Steffie slowed her pace as she entered the room.

Charles stopped talking and his eyes narrowed briefly. "Hello, Stephanie."

"I'll leave you two alone," her father said before Steffie could answer Charles's greeting. He rose, a bit stiffly, and made his way to the door. "I guess you've got plenty to discuss."

Steffie wanted to argue, but realized it wouldn't do any good. She merely shrugged and remained where she was, standing just a few steps from the back stairs. She didn't look at Charles. The silence between them lengthened, until she couldn't endure it any longer.

"I didn't expect you to come," she said in a harsh voice. "It certainly wasn't necessary."

"I'm aware of that."

"I'm not in the mood to go riding and I don't imagine you are, either." It went without saying that she wasn't in the mood to go riding with *him*.

"I'm not here to ride."

"Then why are you here?"

Apparently Charles didn't have the answer because he got to his feet and walked over to the window. Whatever he saw must have fascinated him because he stood there for several moments without saying a word.

"Why are you here?" she asked a second time, ready to request that he leave.

He finally turned around to face her. "I don't know about you, but I couldn't sleep last night."

Steffie refused to admit that she'd fared no better, so she made no response.

"I kept going over the things your father said and the things you told me," Charles went on.

"Did you come to any conclusions?" Pride demanded that she not meet his glance, or reveal how much his answer meant to her.

"One."

Steffie tensed. "What was that?" She had to look at him now.

His eyes burned into hers. Although nearly the entire kitchen separated them, Steffie felt as though he was close enough to touch.

"It seems to me," he began, "that since your father's so anxious to marry you off, and you seem to be just as eager, then fine."

"Fine?" she repeated as though this was some joke and she'd missed the punch line.

"In other words," Charles returned shortly, "I'm willing to take you off his hands."

CHAPTER TEN

"WHAT?"

"Take me off Dad's hands?" Steffie echoed. Surely he wasn't serious. No woman in her right mind would accept such an insulting marriage proposal.

"You heard me."

"Tell me you're kidding."

Charles shook his head. "I've never been more serious in my life. You want to marry me, then so be it. I'm willing to go along with this, provided we understand each other..."

"In that case I withdraw the offer—not that I ever *made* an offer."

"You can't do that," Charles argued, looking surprised. "Your father thinks we should get married and, after giving the matter some thought, I agree with him."

"That's too bad, since I'm not interested."

Charles laughed softly. "We both know that's not true. You've been crazy about me for years."

Steffie whirled around and folded her arms in front of her as though to ward off his words. "I can't marry you, Charles."

"Why not? I know you love me. You said so your-self before you left for Italy, and I know that hasn't changed."

"Don't be so sure."

"Ah, but I am. And recently you let me know it again."

"When?" she demanded, trying to recall the con-versations they'd had since her return to Orchard Valley.

"It was the afternoon we met at Del's."

Steffie cast her mind back to that time. They'd met by accident as they'd gone in to pay for their gas. Steffie remembered how glad she'd been to see him, how eager to set things straight. But she couldn't re-member saying one thing that would lead Charles to believe she still loved him.

"I didn't say anything."

"Not in so many words, true, but with everything you did. The same holds true for the night I dropped off the azalea and you asked me to dinner, remem-ber?"

"Yes, but what's that got to do with anything?"

"A whole lot, as a matter of fact. You were contin-ually making excuses for us to be together."

Steffie's face flooded with color. "What has that got to do with anything?" she demanded again.

He ignored her question. "We had a good time that night, touring Orchard Valley. Didn't we?"

Steffie nodded. She wasn't likely to forget that eve-ning. For the first time in her relationship with Charles, she'd felt a stirring of real promise. Not the kind of hope she'd fabricated three years earlier, but one based on genuine companionship. Charles had enjoyed her company and they'd laughed and talked as though they'd been friends for years.

"You told me that when you lived in Italy you were too busy with your studies to date much," Charles reminded her.

"So?"

"So that led me to conclude that you hadn't fallen in love with anyone else while you were away."

"I hadn't."

"Your father came right out and told me on several occasions that he was concerned about you because you didn't seem to be dating anyone seriously."

Steffie glared at him, feeling trapped. "I still don't know what this has to do with anything."

"Plenty. You loved me then, and you love me now."

"You've got some nerve, Charles Tomaselli." She glowered fiercely, hoping he'd back off. "What makes you so sure I'm in love with you now?"

"I know you better than you realize."

"What nonsense!" She forced a light laugh. "You don't know me at all, otherwise you—" She stopped abruptly.

"Otherwise what?"

"Nothing." *Otherwise he wouldn't have believed the things she'd told him.*

"Don't you think it's time we stopped playing games with each other?" he suggested softly.

"What games?" she snapped. "I gave those up years ago."

Charles frowned as though he wasn't sure he should believe her.

Hurt and angry, Steffie raised her hand and pointed at him. "*That's* the reason I refuse to marry you," she cried. Restraining the emotion was next to impossible and her voice quavered with the force of it. "I suppose I should be flattered that you're willing to take me off Dad's hands," she said sarcastically. "Every woman dreams of hearing such romantic words. But I want far more in a husband, Charles Tomaselli, than you'd ever be capable of giving me!"

"What do you mean by that?" He didn't give her a chance to reply before he muttered, "Oh, I get it. You're afraid I'm going to be financially strapped with the newspaper, aren't you? You think I won't be able to afford you."

Steffie was stunned by his words. Stunned and insulted. "You know me so well, don't you?" she asked him, her voice heavy with scorn. "There's just no pulling the wool over your eyes, is there?" She drew in a deep breath. "I think it would be best if you left." She walked across the kitchen and held open the back door for him. "Right now."

Charles frowned at her and shook his head. "Sorry," he said. "I don't want to leave." He pulled out a chair and threw himself down. "We're going to talk this out, once and for all," he told her.

"Dammit, but you're stubborn."

"So are you."

"We'd make a terrible couple."

"We make a good team."

Steffie didn't know why she was fighting him so hard—especially when he was saying all the things she'd always dreamed of hearing.

"I realize I've made one or two mistakes with this," he said slowly. "It sounded a bit callous, offering to marry you the way I did."

"I'll admit that *taking me off Dad's hands* does lack a certain romantic flair," she agreed wryly. She crossed over to the counter for a coffee mug, filling it from the pot next to the stove. If they were going to talk seriously, without hurling accusations at one another, she was going to need it.

"I was angry."

"Then why'd you come here?" she demanded, claiming the chair across from him.

"Because," he answered in a tight, angry voice, "I was afraid I was going to lose you again."

"Lose me?" That made no sense to Steffie.

"You heard me," he growled. "I was afraid you'd return to Italy or take off on a safari, or go someplace else equally inaccessible."

"Portland. I'm moving to Portland, but it isn't because of what happened with you. I intended to do this from the moment I arrived home." She folded her hands around the hot mug. "Why should you care where I go?"

"Because I didn't want you leaving again."

"Why do you want me to stay, especially if you believe the things I told you yesterday?"

His eyes held hers. "I don't believe them."

"You gave a good impression of it earlier," she reminded him. A fresh wave of pain assaulted her and she looked away.

"That's because I was furious."

"That hasn't changed."

"No, it hasn't," he agreed, "but the simple fact is I don't want you to leave again."

"Unfortunately you don't have any say in what I do."

Charles frowned. "Now you're angry."

"You're damn right I am! Did you honestly think I was so desperate for a husband I'd accept your insulting offer? Is that what you think of me, Charles?"

"No!" he shouted. "I'm in love with you, dammit. I have been for years. I had to do something to keep you here. I don't want to wait another three years for you to come to your senses."

His words were followed by a stunned, disbelieving silence. Steffie stared down into her coffee, and to her chagrin felt tears well up in her eyes. "I'm afraid I don't believe you."

Charles stood abruptly and walked to the window, as he had earlier. Hands clasped behind his back, he gazed outside. "It's true."

"It couldn't be." She wiped the tears from her face. "You were so...so..."

"Cruel," he supplied. "You'll never understand how hard it was not to make love to you that day in the stable. I've never been more tempted by any woman."

"I...tempted you?" Her voice was low and incredulous.

He turned around and smiled, but it was a sad smile, one full of doubts and regrets. "I remember when you first started hanging around the newspaper office. I was flattered by the attention. Soon I found myself looking forward to the times you came by. You were witty and generous and you always had an intelligent comment about something the paper had printed. I quickly discovered you were much more than a pretty face."

"I never worked harder in my life to impress anyone," she murmured with self-deprecating humor.

It didn't take Steffie long to get back to the point in question. "If that was how you felt, then why did you ask me not to come around any longer?"

"I had to say something before I gave in and threw caution to the wind. You'd recently lost your mother and you were young, naive and terribly vulnerable. I struggled with my conscience for weeks, trying to decide what I was going to do about you. In case you haven't noticed, I'm six years older than you. At the time that made a big difference."

"The gap in our ages hasn't narrowed."

"True enough, but you're not a girl anymore."

"I was twenty-one," she argued.

"Perhaps, but you were a sheltered twenty-one. And you were still dealing with your grief. Your entire life had been jolted, and I couldn't be sure if what you felt for me was love or adolescent infatuation."

Steffie closed her eyes and let the warmth of his words revive her. "It was love," she told him softly.

A love that had matured, grown more intense, in the years that separated them.

"I realize it probably doesn't mean much to you now, but I want you to know how hard it was for me the night I came home and found you in my bathtub."

"But you were so angry."

"It was either that or drag you into my room and make love to you."

Steffie remained confused. "You laughed at me when I told you how I felt that day in the stable. . . ."

"I know," he said simply. Steffie heard the pain and remorse in his voice. "I've never had to do anything that's cost me more. But I never dreamed you'd leave Orchard Valley."

"What did you expect me to do? I couldn't stay—that would have been impossible. So I did the only thing I could. I left."

Charles's hand reached for hers, twining their fingers together. "I'll never forget the day I learned you'd gone to Europe. I felt as if I'd been hit by a bulldozer."

"I had to go," she repeated unnecessarily. "It was too painful to stay."

His fingers tightened around hers. "I know." Slowly he raised her hand to his lips. "I've waited three long years to tell you how sorry I was to hurt you. Three years to tell you I was in love with you, too."

Steffie attempted with little success to blink back the tears.

"If it had been at any other time in your life, if I could have been sure you weren't just trying to replace your mother's love with mine—then everything would've been different. But you were so terribly young, so innocent. I couldn't trust myself around you, feeling the way I did."

"And you couldn't trust me."

He nodded his agreement. "I'm sorry, Stephanie, for rejecting you. Just realize that it was as painful for me as it was for you. Perhaps more so, because I knew the whole truth."

"You never wrote—not once in all that time. Not so much as a postcard."

"I couldn't. Believe me, I wanted to, but I didn't dare give in to the impulse. I wasn't sure even then if what you felt for me was genuine love or infatuation."

"So you waited."

"Not patiently. I expected you to come home at least once in three years, you know."

"I dreaded seeing you again. I was thousands of miles away from you and yet I still loved you, I still dreamed about you. It didn't seem to get any better. Even after three years."

"You'd finished your classes and you were in the process of deciding if you were going to stay on in Italy."

"How'd you know that?"

"Your father. He was the only way I had of getting information about you, and I used him shamelessly."

"He told me you started stopping in for visits shortly after I left."

"It's a wonder he didn't figure out how I felt about you. I don't think I could have been any more obvious if I'd tried."

"Dad didn't have a clue until recently and then only because of the—" She stopped when she realized what she was about to tell him.

"Of what?" Charles prodded.

"I . . . it would be best if you let Dad explain that part."

"All right, I will." He looked away from her momentarily. "Although you never seriously dated anyone, there *was* someone in Italy, wasn't there? A man you cared about?"

"Who?" Steffie frowned in bewilderment.

"A man named Mario?"

"Mario . . . a man?" He was four now, and the delight of her heart all the while she'd lived in Italy.

"He gave me several restless nights' worry. Your father only mentioned him once. Said you 'adored' him. I went through the agonies of the damned, trying to be subtle about getting information on this guy, but your father never mentioned him again."

"Mario," Steffie repeated, smiling broadly. "Yes, I did adore him."

Charles scowled. "What happened?"

Still smiling, Steffie said, "There was a slight discrepancy in our ages. I'm about twenty years older."

"He's a kid."

"But what a kid. My landlady's son. I was crazy about him." Spending time with a loving, open child like Mario had helped her though a difficult period in her life.

"I see." A slow, easy smile slipped into place. "So you like children."

"Oh, yes, I always have."

"I hope that young man appreciates all he put me through."

"I'm sure he doesn't, but I certainly do. I know what it's like to love someone and have that someone not love you."

Charles considered her words for several moments. "I've always loved you, Stephanie, but I didn't dare let you know. I couldn't trust what we felt for each other then—but I can now."

She avoided his gaze. She had to ask, though she was afraid to. "If that's true, why were you so angry when Dad suggested we get married?"

Charles sighed. "Frustration, I guess. I'd intended to propose the night we went for dinner. I had everything planned, right down to the last detail."

"But why didn't you?"

"I couldn't, not when the past still came between us. You made it clear you didn't want to discuss our misunderstandings. At least not then. So my hands were tied. I hate to admit it, but I was downright nervous—even if you didn't seem to notice."

"I made it one of my wishes," she recalled, and experienced an instant twinge of regret. Her reluctance to discuss the past had cost her a romantic proposal from the man she loved. It was a lesson she'd remember well.

"That still doesn't explain why you were so offended when Dad suggested we marry." His reaction remained a mystery in light of the things he was telling her now.

"A man prefers to propose himself," Charles offered as a simple explanation. "I don't think I could have made my intentions toward you any plainer had I hired a skywriter, and to have first your father and then you..."

"Me?"

"Yesterday I suddenly felt so afraid that you *weren't* lying about why you'd stopped by at the house. To put in the finishing blow, to get me to admit I loved you and then laugh at me..."

"I—I made that part up! You made me so mad—"

"I made you mad?" he cried.

"I know, I know. It's just that I had to say something. I didn't think you'd believe all those ridiculous lies, and then you seemed to and that made everything a thousand times worse. I was just beginning to hope we might have a future together."

"I was, too. That's why it hit me so hard."

"I could never intentionally hurt you, Charles. Not without hurting myself."

His eyes held hers, and everything around Steffie faded into significance. She was on the verge of disclosing all the love in her heart when there was a knock at the kitchen door, followed by her father poking his head inside. "Is it safe yet? You two looked like time bombs about to explode twenty minutes ago."

"It's safe," Charles answered, smiling at Steffie.

"I hope you've got everything worked out because I'm getting tired of waiting. The way I figure it, you should be married by the end of the summer. Your oldest—"

"Dad," Steffie cut in. "I don't think Charles is interested in discussing it right now. Why don't you leave all of that to us?"

"Our oldest?" Charles asked, frowning.

"Child, of course. A girl, followed by a son and then another daughter. Sweethearts, all three of them. The boy will be the spitting image of you, Charles— same dark brown eyes, same facial features."

Charles glanced at Steffie as though he wasn't sure of her father's sanity.

"I think you'd better tell Charles about the dream, Dad."

"You mean you haven't?" He sounded surprised.

"No, I didn't want to frighten the dear man out of marrying into the family."

"What's going on here?" Charles's gaze roved from Steffie to her father and back.

"I'm not sure you're going to believe this," David said, pulling out a chair and settling himself. He grinned, happy as Steffie could ever remember seeing him. "But I got a glimpse of the future. It was a gift from Grace. She wanted to be sure I had a reason to live and so she had me—"

"But isn't Grace—"

"She's in heaven, but then so was I, briefly. It was what they call a near-death experience. You can ask Colby about this if you don't believe me."

"Colby?" Charles repeated.

"I'm not convinced he believes me one hundred percent, but time will prove me right. Look at what's happened with Valerie and Colby, just the way I said it would. And with you two, for that matter. You're going to marry this little girl of mine, aren't you?"

"In a heartbeat," Charles confirmed.

Her father's grin split his face. "That's what I thought. You love him, don't you, Princess?"

Steffie nodded. "More than I thought it was possible to love anyone," she said in a hushed voice.

David smiled knowingly and eased himself out of his chair. "In that case, I'll leave you two to discuss the details of your wedding. I'd like to suggest midsummer, but as I said, I'll leave that up to you." He slipped out of the room.

"Midsummer?" Steffie repeated.

"Sounds good to me. Does that give you enough time?"

She laughed. "Sure, and I'll be able to register for my courses, according to plan—if that's okay with you?" At his enthusiastic agreement, she added, "Uh...what do you think about Dad's dream?"

"A boy and two girls, he says."

Steffie nodded shyly.

"How do *you* feel about that?" he asked.

"Good, very good. How about you?"

Charles reached for her then, wrapping her in his arms with the strength of a man who'd been too long without love. He buried his face in the gentle curve of her neck and breathed deeply. "I nearly lost you for the second time."

"You'd never have lost me, Charles. I've loved you for so long, I don't know how not to love you." He'd been a part of her for so many years that she couldn't imagine continuing without him now.

"I love you, Stephanie. Give me a chance to prove it."

In her eyes, he'd already proved it when he hadn't laughed at her father's dream. She knew what he was thinking, perhaps because she was thinking the same thing herself. They were in love, had already decided to marry, so it didn't matter what her father had predicted after his supposed sojourn in the afterlife. It was the course they'd willingly set for themselves.

He kissed her then, and her heart seemed to overflow with love, just as her eyes overflowed with tears.

"Stephanie," Charles whispered, his lips against hers. "We have a lot of time to make up for."

"It'll take at least fifty years, won't it?"

"At the very least," he murmured, kissing her again with a need that left her breathless.

DAVID BLOOMFIELD relaxed in his rocker on the front porch, his smile one of utter contentment. It was coming to pass, just as he'd known it would. Just as

Grace had told him. First Valerie, and now Steffie. His grin widened.

My heavens, he thought, Norah was in for one wallop of a surprise.

*   *   *   *   *

Who's the man for Norah? Next month, find out if David's right about his youngest daughter's future. Norah, *Book 3 of Debbie Macomber's Orchard Valley trilogy. Harlequin Romance #3244*

HARLEQUIN®

THE TAGGARTS OF TEXAS!

Harlequin's Ruth Jean Dale brings you
THE TAGGARTS OF TEXAS!

Those Taggart men—strong, sexy and hard to resist...

You've met Jesse James Taggart in FIREWORKS!
Harlequin Romance #3205 (July 1992)

And Trey Smith—he's THE RED-BLOODED YANKEE!
Harlequin Temptation #413 (October 1992)

Now meet Daniel Boone Taggart in SHOWDOWN!
Harlequin Romance #3242 (January 1993)

And finally the Taggarts who started it all—in LEGEND!
Harlequin Historical #168 (April 1993)

Read all the Taggart romances!
Meet all the Taggart men!

Available wherever Harlequin Books are sold.

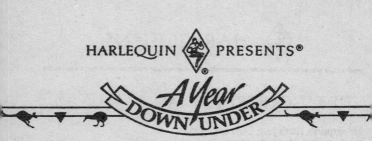